BRE GARCIA

Jackrabbit and the Beast

A Jackrabbit Brujo Tale

First published by Bre Garcia 2023

Copyright © 2023 by Bre Garcia

This novel is entirely a work of fiction. The names, characters and incidents portrayed in it are the work of the author's imagination. Any resemblance to actual persons, living or dead, events or localities is entirely coincidental.

Bre Garcia asserts the moral right to be identified as the author of this work.

First printed in Bellingham, WA, by Village Books

First edition

ISBN (print): 979-8-9894800-2-9
ISBN (digital): 979-8-9894800-1-2

This book was professionally typeset on Reedsy.
Find out more at reedsy.com

For Hnue
Thank you for your undying support

1

Laura was dead and his hand was up her best friend's shirt. Or perhaps it would be better to say his girlfriend was dead and his hand was up their mutual friend's shirt. Or perhaps it was all mush anyway because he didn't remember getting there and he wouldn't remember leaving either.

It was exactly one month since her funeral. Vel had been counting the days, though not because he was calculating when it would be appropriate to move in on his dead girlfriend's best friend. He was simply counting. Counting because time passed by like sludge and yet every time he blinked it would be a week later. Four blinks meant a month, and at the end of those four blinks he was in Shoua's apartment with a bottle of beer clutched clumsily in his hand. Shoua had been nursing her own drink, and that wine clashed with the beer in his breath when they sloppily kissed. Sloppy, yes. Desperate and hard. He missed Laura.

A lot.

Six years ago Laura, in her nigh-divine consistency to mistake left and right, had stepped into the path of his bicycle. The result of the crash had left her with a pinched cut on her leg and a sprained ankle. There were bruises on his legs from trying to quickly untangle himself from the bike, but he hardly remembered them. He remembered helping her to the side, joking that it would've been funnier if he had left a cartoonish tire print on her skin instead, and she laughed at that. A day later her bruises looked just so, and for reasons he didn't quite understand she suggested a date. On that date Vel had teased her for asking him out at all, and Laura's response expressed a loving interest in coincidence. That charmed him.

Now she was dead, and in the wake of the funeral he was remembering more and more details of that day; reliving it until the angle of the sun was perfect, the exact type of bright warmth, the sounds of their shoes scuffing the pavement. The unique sensation of hearing her voice for the first time, not knowing and yet somehow predicting he'd hear it again and again in different tones and pitches. From groggy sick croaks to impassioned lilts, her voice sank in his mind. Similarly, her blue eyes, her straw-blonde hair, the particular temperature of her waist under his hand, the quirks of her words, the flexibility of her beliefs, over and over again he remembered her. All the while, Shoua moved with him on the couch with equal measures of listlessness and despair.

If Laura could see them now, she wouldn't believe it. To call Vel and Shoua mutual friends was not quite a lie, but not quite a truth either. They existed comfortably in their own spaces, hurling cheery insults and annoyances at one another. Vel enjoyed getting under her skin, Shoua enjoyed being angry about it, and vice versa. Laura was their fulcrum, and without her it, well. It was mush. Filthy, shameful, pained mush.

Suddenly Shoua wriggled in a way that broke the rhythm. Vel shifted his long arm first to adjust, then reluctantly to pull away and let her free. She slipped from under him and hurried herself to the bathroom. He heard the distinct click of the lock, a sound that hit him in the head.

He had fucked up, and he had fucked up bad. Shoua let him in because he was half-drunk with sorrow anyway, and *really* he shouldn't have come here because on top of Laura she was dealing with a break-up. Hell, it might've been because of Laura's death. It might've been because Vel had become such a distant, hollow mess that Shoua took up much of his part at the funeral. Break-ups happened over lesser burdens.

So who was he, anyway, to barge in like this and cry on her couch moments before kissing and fondling thoughtlessly? Well. No taking it back. No taking it back, no taking Laura back, no taking six years of his life back. With great effort Vel pushed himself up, dragging his long limbs until he was curled drunkenly on the opposite end of the couch. Pathetically, his dick still throbbed. Through hoarse, weak laughs, Vel briefly thought he should just take care of it there in Shoua's living room. Fuck it, right? He'd already gone this far. What was just a little bit more? Nothing mattered.

Graciously through the power of depression, he did nothing but push his eyes into the crook of his elbow hard enough to keep the tears squeezed thin.

Softly the lock clicked again and Shoua emerged, though she stood at the threshold between hallway and living room and did not enter again. She was short, extremely so, a mere four-foot-ten if she wasn't wearing her boots. He had never in his life felt like she could tower over him, but when he pulled his face out of his arm and glanced over, she could've been his height. Taller. Impossibly tall, from so far away.

"I'm...sorry, Vel," her voice was meek, and it gutted him. He'd rather hear her shout and swear, "Maybe if...,"

She paused, thinking and thinking hard. Black lipstick disappeared into her mouth and reappeared with pink toothmarks underneath, "It's...weird, right." she said it like a statement and a question at the same time, "It's weird."

He looked away to the coffee table where his near-empty beer bottle stood next to her cleared out wine glass. It *was* weird. Yet it still hurt to hear and it sounded like Shoua was all too aware of that.

Vel made a noise that was hard to describe, but at least it sounded like him. At least he had that, because he had to re-measure himself in Laura's absence. What made it worse was that there was no returning to who he was six years prior, and no moving forward without acknowledging Laura had been there in the first place. He stood up to go home for chrissakes—the home they had bought together two years prior. Since her death he got flashes of anxiety; the mortgage, the ownership, life insurance, all things to be dealt with later. Later. Later, after this. Hopefully never.

He wobbled on his feet. It was so hard to go home.

"Vel," Shoua had finally re-entered the living room, "How much have you had tonight?"

Vel grunted, "Not that much."

Shoua raised an eyebrow as he caught his balance against the coffee table, clinking the glasses on it. He grimaced.

"Are you sure?" she pressed.

"Yes." Really, the alcohol wasn't the problem here.

Suddenly Shoua grabbed his arm. The beads around his wrist clacked as she sharply tugged to assert her authority. Her voice too had turned sharp, and he felt a pang of emotion swell in his chest. This was what he needed, Shoua acting normal, no different, like nothing had happened at all.

"Vel." the hard edges of her voice hit and he felt himself on the verge of crying, "I'm serious. I don't—I don't want another funeral so...so soon."

"I'm fine, Boots." he croaked. The use of his nickname for her had its intended effect, and Shoua slowly let go of him. He shook his wrist to hear the beads clack again, bobbed his head as if nodding (but really to keep the tears at bay), and swallowed hard, "Um. Uh...,"

For once, she was patient, even though her arms were crossed. "Thanks. Y'know."

Shoua opened her mouth to reply, but when nothing came out she closed it again. The last detail he noticed was that she readjusted her grip on her arms, tighter, as if she was trying not to shake.

Vel opened the door and stepped out from her basement apartment into the cooling desert air. He could feel Shoua's eyes at his back, calculating and vigilant. A spike of defiance kept him upright from the familiarity of fighting back against her. However he did it, he managed to keep Shoua's concerns well enough at bay to get into his old sedan, start the engine, swallow down the tears, and back out of the apartment driveway.

Tucson at night swept by as he drove. Glowing oranges blurred in his vision. It's fine. He knew the way home by heart by now. Many times picking Laura up after a night out with Shoua, many times driving back after failing to plan the funeral. Vel put his hand at the top of the wheel as he dug out a cigarette. He had picked it up as a rebellious habit in high school, making his tía rave endlessly in Spanish about how terrible it was. After he moved out the habit slid off, and after Laura he had quit all together.

Vel pulled the lighter he had stolen from the same tía's end table and lit the cigarette. The smoke coupled with the night air calmed him. No, it didn't really. But it took the mush and defined it with edges, and that was enough to keep him going a little while longer. He thumbed the leather case the lighter was in, well worn by both his and he supposed his tía's hand over the years. An embossed eagle wreathed with flowers still pressed against his restless thumb.

He turned into his driveway and forgot how he got there, as he had known he would. Things sloughed to the floor as he moved through the house, shoes, socks, shirt. Even his wooden jewelry he tossed carelessly on the bathroom counter, pitching himself over the sink like he was in pain.

The mirror greeted him horribly. His droopy eyes were sunken in dark circles even though all he could remember of the past several days was sleeping. For half a second he saw a pale hand in his peripherals, reaching to brush the sparse, prickly stubble on his jaw. Laura would remark something about how terrible he looked, how he needed rest, but before he fell into the fantasy a frustrated anger boiled in him. He *had* been resting. He had been doing nothing *but* resting. The result was this strange creature in front of him. This strange creature with a vacant space at his chest, with no blonde head of hair to rest his chin upon. She had been the perfect height for that. His nose was big and stuck out, all the better to nuzzle her with in the morning.

Vel wiped his thumb against where his lips were on the mirror, then in a moment struck with shame realized he was trying to wipe smudges of Shoua's black lipstick off his face. The shame became brutalized, and the next moments went by in a frenzy. Sink water hissing, hands rubbing harsh, then washcloth, more water, more abrasion—his chapped lips were not pleased with him.

When it was all said and done, there was still a vacancy beneath his chin. He dropped his gaze to the streaks of lipstick now in the washcloth, and a related kind of shame swelled in him. His eyes hurt, stung, then felt overly warm. He should, he wished he could apologize to Shoua.

Instead he slumped on his side of the bed, turned, grasped at nothing, and because of Shoua he thought about the raw act of kissing. About how this bed had become home more than the house itself, a place to bury his smile in Laura. His dick recovered its hardness and Vel bit his dry lips. It took longer, so much longer, and at one point he had stopped all together because his face was buried in her pillow to cry. But eventually he spent himself over her side of the bed, and eventually he fell asleep.

* * *

His phone rang. Mercifully he had long ago changed the ring tone to something generic and wooden, far from emotional associations. But he still groaned. After a few failed attempts to retrieve it he pressed the screen to his ear and grunted in place of words.

"Vel. I need you at a scene."

Chrissake. It was the lieutenant—Lieu, as he called her. No-nonsense, called him for consultations on tricky and untoward cases where her stalwart basic approaches turned up nothing. Vel scowled into the pillow and scrunched his eyes so tight he saw spots.

"You weren't up? It's almost noon." her voice was curt and

emotionless—it would've downright been accusatory had he not known the lieutenant for so long he could recognize the concern. Concern from her, of course, only came in word choice. But it was concern nonetheless.

"Can't you call in someone else?" he complained. He'd like to say it was his attempt at a joke. There was *no* one else to call if Lieu was calling him. But seriously, for real, he wished for once there had been someone, anyone else. There probably was, but, much as she wouldn't admit it, Lieu had a soft spot for him. The line went silent save for the milling of officers in the background.

"...No." she was not impressed, and she did not laugh.

Vel sighed, "Fine. Where?"

If they were trying to conceal the crime scene from the trailhead they weren't doing a very good job, but then Lieu had said it'd be easy to find. Like, you know, barring the cop cars that didn't want to get more dust and rock scratches than usual on their SUVs. There was an officer up front before the start of the perimeter to turn people away, and Vel, in the V-neck he wore the day before with unwashed jeans, approached him thoughtlessly. To make matters worse, he had a backpack slung over one shoulder. Saying that the officer eyed him suspiciously would be a deeply softened lie.

"This is a crime scene. No civilians past this point."

No 'sir', no greetings. Vel planted his feet a bit hard at a distance that should've been safe but with his height and limbs it wasn't. He tried neutrality, "Can you tell Lieutenant K that Vel is here?"

The officer was unimpressed, "Lieutenant who?"

Annoyance gurgled in his gut. He should've slept in, more, longer. Stayed inside, "Kulasiewicz. Tell her I'm here."

"Can't do that until you give me your name."

"Vel."

"Don't play smug with me."

He let out a frustrated sigh, "Velasquez." The officer didn't budge. Vel grew tart, "Jerónimo Velasquez. Let me through."

The officer didn't acknowledge him as he took his time scribbling down his name in his notebook. Vel pursed his lips, then tipped forward in his cowboy boots.

"No, man. N then M, Jerónimo."

The officer snapped his notebook shut and snarled up at Vel, "I could have you arrested for prying into a police investigation if you want to play *games*,"

"Well can you at least spell my name right? Don't want to arrest the wrong guy now, officer,"

"Final warning. Don't play smug, or I'll—,"

"Officer Johnson," Vel felt tension release as Lieu climbed up over the rocky ridge. She brushed herself off as she talked, hair in a tight bun and eyes hidden behind sunglasses, "Thank you for notifying me that our consultant arrived."

He had not, but the look on his face was furious. Vel allowed himself a lopsided, *very* smug smile, and was surprised with how easy it had been to do.

"And Vel, can you *try* to be nice?"

"I am nice. I play nice." he protested in a flat tone. Lieu sighed. He thought of a million more things to say; that *it's not my fault that I prod your officers until they snap, it's his fault he started it mom, is it because I'm brown?* But all fell by the wayside, shriveled before they left his tongue. Her head was perked as though she expected more from him too, but at his strange silence simply led him to the body.

Lieu was a stern woman, with hair that grayed on the top

as it stayed a sandy brown beneath. He had first met her a little over a decade ago when he was still in high school. It was not...the easiest time to think about, but he couldn't deny that Lieu covered for him when she had no reason to. She had come off as a strict, by-the-numbers, hard evidence type, so the fact that she had any faith to place at all—much less in him—was baffling. Lieu took facts at face value and never shared anything vulnerable if she believed it to be self-evident anyways—which it almost always was to her. How, in the storm of her ruthlessness, she had decided that he was a viable hire for consultation would remain forever a mystery. Vel was nosy in more ways than one, but Lieu was locked up so tight even he couldn't weasel his way in.

"This is the fourth of its kind. Female, young, multiple blunt cuts to the front of the body likely from an axe—,"

Vel winced, but continued following Lieu as she spoke.

"—dumped sometime last night, found by hikers this morning as they were going up the trail. We've already questioned and sent them home, and they didn't say anything that we can't already see. Time of death over a day ago, but hasn't been exposed to the elements until recent."

She paused, something Vel didn't notice until she took up what he should've said in the interim.

"So, she wasn't killed here, that is certain. What's left of her blood already pooled at the bottom; she was stored in likely the same position as she was found."

There she was, laying face up in the desert. Her body was skewed around the rocks. Glazed, open eyes stared up at the sun, baked still and expressionless. The face was untouched and her clothes were still on, but the farther down her body the less it mattered. Lieu's voice retained its hardened edge, albeit with a solemn respect.

"No signs of sexual assault, but with the state of her lower half we should wait for what the coroner says."

"Uh-huh," Vel finally said, dropping his backpack to the ground, "And you called me because...you don't know where to go, right."

She sighed and even that sounded curt, "Right. No strange stuff." Vel nodded and rifled through his bag. Dowsing rod wouldn't work, there's no blood to trail. No strange stuff should've been easy but that meant he had less to latch onto. He shouldn't complain, it usually wasn't a big deal at all, but he felt like he had to. He felt like he should, that he was *owed* to complain. Vel didn't realize that Lieu was carefully scrutinizing him until she said, "You look bad, Vel."

"Love you too, Lieu," he grunted, swallowing a rock in his throat when the first word came back around to haunt him.

"Are you hungover?"

"Had a couple of drinks. Drove fine."

"Are you high?"

He looked up in indignant surprise. What the hell sort of question was that? Hallucinogens did not mix well with him and she knew it. Even if he wasn't on deck to take a job, it made him anxious in very unfun ways no matter the strain. He had explained this to her many times before, but her expression was stone-still and serious.

She repeated herself as an explanation, "You look *bad*, Vel. Did you look in the mirror before you left?"

He rubbed his face and gazed into his bag as if he could see himself in it. Well, he could take note of how he felt; his eyes were tired and strained, so perhaps they were reddened too. His head felt a little woozy—perhaps he *was* hungover but it felt no different than a recent day where he hadn't drunk anything. Did that mean his gait was unbalanced too? Already he was trying to write it off as *you don't have limbs like tree branches you wouldn't know how hard it is to keep upright*, but Lieu rarely, if ever, minced words. So she was probably right.

No wonder the harsh scrutiny from the officer at the perimeter.

"...Perhaps you should go—,"

"I'm fine." he interrupted, rubbing his hands on his knees and looking in the general direction—but just past—the body.

"Vel,"

"Hey I need to get out," he rushed the words, "Need to. Pay bills and eat and get out and get back to work and—,"

"I agree," she said it, and said it in such a way that his heart wrenched. She hadn't called him out here for help. She called him out here because it was her way of trying to get him back in the saddle, "But maybe not for this case."

She looked where he was looking, but almost certainly she was setting her gaze on the body in full, "I'm sorry, Vel."

It was Lieu. All she saw was a girl killed by an axe murderer. Perhaps it had crossed her mind that the blood, the cuts, the wounds were localized in the same area as Laura's. But because Laura was torn up, shredded by some brutish wild animal, it was different in her mind. This girl was murdered. Laura was simply killed.

Granted, he shouldn't have said yes. He should've put his foot down and stayed home in the sheets he had dirtied, wallowing. But Lieu, for as much as this was her gesture to help him, didn't call without reason. They really *were* stuck, enough that she could suggest bringing him in. Vel remained motionless, the body blurring in favor of the rocks in his vision. Lieu told him to leave again.

An idea perked in his head and he shook it and grabbed the dowsing rod. Maybe it *would* work, just not in the way he had first figured. With Lieu's voice behind him, he gingerly crawled to the poor girl without acknowledgment.

"Hey, you get your pics already?" he asked the photographer. Vel didn't exactly know the names of the lackeys Lieu carried around, but this wasn't his first crime scene. Some recognized him, and he vaguely knew them in turn. The photographer merely nodded, tossed him a pair of gloves, and gestured for him to do his thing.

His thing was different every time, but it didn't matter. Vel knelt near the girl in what would've surely been a pool of her blood had it been the actual place she died. Lieu's voice had stopped, but he felt her standing a respectable distance behind him, watching.

Alright. Alright.

"Hey there sunshine," Vel cooed to the frozen face, "I'd like to borrow some of your blood for a sec, if that's alright." He started digging a hole to the side that was narrow enough to push a pole into. Shoring up its foundation with rocks, he pulled the dowsing rod out of his backpack.

"I won't have to go deep," he promised while nudging a wound farther open. It was difficult, the skin had already lost its elasticity. Vel grimaced, biting his lips and blinking rapidly. Bodies were never particularly *easy* to deal with on an emotional level, but all of his walls and doors were broken right now; there was no retreating to a space in his mind that could detach. She was around Vel's age, late twenties, put together enough to likely have a significant other or maybe even a family. Maybe she had a degree, or was just about to finish one, or had gone to work right out of school. No, degree was more likely, there were less signs of hard labor on her than he would expect otherwise. He swallowed hard. Rigor mortis had already begun to break down into secondary relaxation, but he didn't want to shove things in where they didn't belong. He was no coroner.

Still, he managed himself enough to dip the dowsing rod into her belly, wind it up like a q-tip, and pull away.

"There, done for now," Vel promised, then apologized twice. One, "I'm so sorry", in gratitude for allowing his intrusion. Then another, slower, "I'm so sorry" for this having happened at all.

Vel popped the dowsing rod on top of the pole he stuck in the ground, tested it for its looseness, and let it sit as he examined the body further. Lieu remained behind him, quiet.

"Lieu, you caught this right?" Vel called over his shoulder as he raised the girl's hand by his fingertips, "Car grease?"

"Yes. But no car or identification yet."

Huh. There wasn't a lot of grease, maybe just enough that she was checking the engine or poking around the dipsticks. Whatever it had been, she had not had enough time to wipe it off. But generally when checking a car for trouble the backside would be exposed, not the front. Either she was attacked in between checking and finishing up or she was interrupted.

The dowsing rod jerked. Vel looked over. It remained still, jerked again, then slowly moved in a quarter of an arc. The bottom half that rested on the pole nudged forward as if being pulled by something. It slacked. It pulled forward again then turned left. Once it was reoriented it was pulled forward again. The pull loosened, then stopped. Vel waited a few moments. The dowsing rod then pulled, slowed, turned, pulled again.

"Vel?" Lieu asked for an explanation. He tapped his leg

anxiously and pulled out his phone. When the rod stopped again he hit the timer. After nearly eighty seconds, it moved. Frowning, he stared at the number.

Lieu stepped forward and he scratched the barbed stubble on his jaw, "Got good news for you. Think I figured out where she was murdered,"

"Where?" Lieu said, "How?"

"Well, there's bad news too. She was murdered in a car or a truck or something," he gestured to the still moving dowsing rod, "One that's working perfectly fine. Probably going out for lunch."

What Lieu didn't need to know was that this had not exactly gone as he had planned. All he had wanted and hoped to get from the dowsing rod was the general direction of where she was murdered which—technically it gave him. On one hand it was better than telling Lieu *that way* and pointing with utmost lunacy as though he did anything but trust a stiff breeze. On the other, it was going to be hell tracking down a moving target.

"So uh," Vel croaked, standing up and brushing himself off, "Good luck with that."

Honestly, he was depressed enough to stop off at a Taco Bell. Mentioning lunch at the crime scene hit him with a wave of hunger crushed with a nauseating lack of appetite, but he had to eat *somehow*. Not being able to recall anything but the beers from last night was not a good sign, no matter how nauseated he was. He rubbed his gurgling stomach and pulled into the first thing that sounded good *before* he wound up at a Taco Bell. Gorditas were more than welcome enough.

The stout cooks behind the counter greeted him in Spanish and asked what he would like. That's what it sounded like, anyway. He swallowed hard enough that his voice cracked when he spoke, "Uh, hi yeah. Pibil and...the mushroom one. Two of each. Thanks."

The workers transitioned to English smoothly enough, but every time this happened—often—he swore he could see a little light die in their eyes. Most days it was just a little awkwardness, maybe embarrassment, but today it garnered guilt, and he sputtered out a pathetic *gracias* when he took his food. Something always felt wrong when he said it, not fluent enough, not natural, he rolled the R too much or not enough. Maybe it was more common than he thought, but for as much as he loved his mother he often questioned why she had not raised him with both languages.

Not that it had been easy for her. She had been undocumented, crossing the border while pregnant with him. On top of that, she had been alone. If she was going to be caught, having him only speak English would surely protect him in the long run—away from the gruesome persecutions she was fleeing from. At least, that was her logic. Something *had* caught up with her when he was twelve and left her dead on the floor. Since he was still around she must've been right.

By the time his tía raised him in the wake of her death, it felt too late. Of course, that didn't stop her from yelling at him in Spanish when she was pissed. It rarely affected him. If English would go in his teenage ear and out the other, Spanish flew far above his head and didn't look back.

What could his tía do in any sense of the term, though? It had been the first time he had seen a dead body, half cut by shadow that mercifully masked the gore of her murder. The part of her that was lit by light from the door frame remained etched in his nightmares, her outstretched fist clutching something he couldn't see. She was cold when he reached forward to pry her hand open, no longer warmed by flipping tortillas on the comal.

In her hand were her eyes, clawed out by her own fingers and kept safe. They gazed up at him as if waiting for his arrival, sad and pining to hold and tell him it was alright. Whatever had possessed him that night he didn't know, but he knew his mother's quirks and beliefs were important. The eyes must've been important too. He took them in his pocket, held them when the police scoured his house, held them when his tía signed the adoption papers. They never decayed or dried, really—not in the way bodies should. Holding them felt like they had been glass eyes all along, though they had some give and leeched the warmth from his hand like it gave them life enough to see again.

They rested in a case at the base of the ofrenda in the spare bedroom—unopened and unknown to anyone except to him. He didn't suppose he had ever told Laura, or that he would ever have had occasion to. Laura knew of the accusations that his mother was a witch and accepted his odd inclinations towards the undefined occult because of it, but he had not told her that he went so far as to keep her eyes. The strangest milagro, Santa Lucía's blessing of a dead bruja mother.

Going to Taco Bell and talking to the high teenager working the register would not surface these kinds of memories like this. He should've gone there instead.

Vel nestled himself in the corner and sulked into the gorditas.

Five minutes later the door opened and to his shock and dismay, Lieu walked in. She had a folder under her arm, and upon locating him in the corner, took her sunglasses off and sat down across from him.

"I would ask if you're stalking me, but since you're a cop I guess that's kind of a given, huh?"

She let out a terse breath of exasperation and put the folder on the table, "You left without the case file." an invisible *idiot* hung after her sentence–a word she'd never say to him, but oh, implied many times.

"Yeah I mean," he covered for himself, because he *had* totally forgotten to take it, "You told me to leave."

"And you didn't listen. So now you're involved in the case."

"Where can I turn in my badge and gun?"

"I'm glad you don't have either."

"Jesus, Lieu," he spoke into a gordita, "I'm sensitive right now."

She stared at him, her gray eyes cold and stony as ever. Not only was his voice far too flat and flippant to be sincere, but he had not once, ever, expressed interest in joining the force. To say such a thing after years of Vel pestering her to quit and be an underpaid loser with him in the private investigation field, well, he wasn't fooling her. Didn't make her laugh either, though by his marks a smirk counted as a laugh from Lieu.

"If you want to withdraw you are free to do so. But you have a hard time letting things go–," Lieu had begun the sentence with a sigh that she sucked back in upon the unintentional barbs thrown at him, but he let it be. From anyone else it would be too pointed an attack, from Lieu it was normal, "–which means I'm expecting you to see this through."

He chewed to give the impression he was thinking. (He was not.) As he pretended to think he reached with his other hand and offered a mushroom gordita to her.

"Would you like one?"

Lieu scrunched her nose, "No."

Vel pouted in a spectacular display, "You don't want a gordita?"

Lieu fixed her gaze on him, "No."

"You don't want a dark slimy gooey texture in an appetizing green sauce that—," he squished it for good measure, "—sounds just as good as it looks?"

"*Vel*,"

"No mushroom chubbies?"

Lieu, known mushroom–hater, gave a harsher sigh than before. He watched with a spark of delight—so rare these days—as she massaged her temples so deeply they left red marks on her skin. She did not look back at him until he put the damn thing down. As an apology and a retreat, he presented the remaining pibil one.

"You don't want that?" she asked.

"...No." he answered, and the sincerity in his voice—the meek, tired, ashamed admission of his lack of appetite—made Lieu take the offer.

Wiping his fingers clumsily on his shirt, he reached for the file. Lieu slapped her hand on it.

"Vel, there are *pictures*,"

"I'm in the corner!" he protested like a petulant kid. Defiantly he slid it out from under her hand and flipped it open. At the *very* least, he held one side up to protect the information within. That hardly mattered, but it wasn't worth fighting about right now.

Four women, scattered across the past several months, all killed with axe blows to the lower half. Mindlessly he ate the next gordita (the one he had teased Lieu with), more to distract himself than to battle his ruined appetite. Each girl had been dumped near trailheads or similar wilderness with minimal attempt to hide the bodies. Another bite that he didn't taste. They were also all white, which made the attacks seem targeted instead of random. The curiosity that stood out the most to him though was the time frame between the third and fourth woman. There were approximately six weeks in between each body being killed and found, but between the third and fourth it had inexplicably doubled to twelve. Six weeks had seemed enough for them to evade police capture. It was not an exact science, but if the killer had a pattern then this recent victim should've been the fifth. Had they almost been caught and played it safe? Or...

He sniffed, finding his hand empty of a gordita he didn't remember finishing, "What do you think?"

"I assume the killer is male," Lieu provided. Vel didn't

dissent and simply flipped from picture to picture clipped to each respective file. All were clothed. The first three women had no clear signs of sexual assault, though the coroner noted it was difficult to tell with their lower halves in such a state. And really, searching for semen in their remains in order to label at such was splitting hairs on what sexual assault meant in the first place. With the force used and the destructive violence it had to have been on the killer's mind.

"What about the gap between this and the last girl?"

"Hm?" Lieu leaned forward. Vel shrugged.

"Seems a bit large compared to the others, is all. No missed bodies between now and then right?"

Lieu thought for a moment, "The first was found in late January. The second in early March, then mid-April."

"And now the jump to mid-July. What, did they go on vacation or something?"

Lieu's lips pressed thin in thought, "Spring is busy for hikers. They would've been more likely to be caught then."

"Not if they dumped them in the dead of night, though—like they seem to do.

"True. Perhaps."

It was always *perhaps* until they were *correct*, and even then correctness almost never came. Vel found himself staring a little too hard at one of the gruesome photos and felt the nausea return. He carefully shut the file and slid his hand down to flatten it.

"...You didn't really need my help today, did you?" Vel asked, direct and quiet. Even though directness was Lieu's comfort zone, she did not answer right away.

"You helped." she finally settled on, firm as though she was ensuring he wouldn't misunderstand.

The line between the beige folder and the browned copper color of his hand blurred, not from tears but from a catatonic-like stare that he couldn't shake himself from. Laura had been found like those girls. Blood had led the hikers to her, a frenetic trail as though what had killed her had dragged her kicking and screaming through the rocky sand. It coagulated into disgusting garnets in the early summer sunlight. Sprays of blood painted the saguaro her body was wrapped around, and he wondered if in her final moments she embraced it for protection and comfort. Anything was better, kinder, than what had torn her apart.

She had been out with Shoua that night, no different than normal. *Girl's night, not planning to get too drunk so I'll be okay to drive.* He recalled his last words to her, the cadence, the teasing, the shit that would haunt him because it was far too flippant and insincere for their final moments. *What, not gonna get wild and crazy without me? I'm hurt.* Laura laughed, stood up on her tiptoes to kiss his cheek (that he bent down for her to be able to reach). They said *love you,* flippant, punctuated, short, too routine to mean anything.

Not gonna get wild and crazy without me?

No, Shoua had said the next morning with concern creeping into her voice. Laura had left normally last night, she should've been home well before midnight even.

Vel. This is not...that kind of call. Lieu didn't greet him when he picked up the phone. Lieu didn't mince words. Lieu hesitated. *I'm sorry.*

I'm hurt.

She should've driven straight home. The dents in her car were severe but she would've had to have been stopped for them to be made. No real impact damage. It was found abandoned on the side of the road, not anywhere near where her body had been.

"Vel. *Vel.*"

"Uh-huh." he answered on reflex. Lieu snapped her fingers under his nose, brusque and sharp. He blinked, "I said yeah."

"I didn't ask a question."

He looked dumb at the table like he didn't recognize where he was, "Oh."

Lieu leaned back to get a good look at him, and he slouched. Her eyes drifted to the file on the table.

"I made a mistake, Vel. You have the files if you want to continue, but I won't plan on calling you again. Not for this, anyway."

"They're different though," he weakly protested, "No blood trail, there's an axe, uh...,"

"Are they?" Lieu skewered him.

He looked down at the closed file and blurted, "The time that Laura's body was found fits the in the gap between the third and fourth girls."

Lieu stared, and for a few horrifying minutes he was afraid she'd yank the folder from under his hand, strip him of his job title (as if she had that power—or at least she could say she'd never hire him again) and coldly leave him alone in the gordita shop. Her fingers pressed on the edges of the folder like she was about to do just that, but after a long, long contemplation she released it and stood up.

"You have the file, but I can't take your suggestions seriously while you're like this. Go home."

She turned to leave and he felt kicked to the side of the road.

"Lieu—," he called, and mercifully she stopped, "...Your gordita."

She took it with little to no acknowledgment and left. Vel sat, staring at the closed folder. Then, somehow, he scraped himself together. Again. He wrapped the last gordita in wax paper the best he could. Even if the tortilla got soggy in his fridge, the fillings would be salvageable for another meal. Not *part* of another meal, he knew, but another meal all together.

The air was blisteringly hot when he left, the middle of the afternoon having reached its peak. For those that took siestas, they would start to move again as the temperature slowly eased downwards. Still, his car was insufferable, and he took his chances with the window open to at least blow air in his face before the A/C kicked in. Laura's Jeep had always been the better of the two. It had been cleaner, didn't smell of smoke, didn't have a rosary wrapped thrice around the rearview so he wouldn't get pulled over for it swinging in the way—again. Sometimes in his frustration after her death he wanted to punt the car into a junkyard. Buy a Jeep, pretend she was still there, go deeper into denial than keeping his twenty-year-old sedan on life support.

He pulled out a cigarette. Why had Laura left her car? If the animal that attacked her had been hurt, maybe she would— but if it had been large enough she would've stayed inside and called animal control. They would further advise her to stay safe, and kind as she was she would've driven home once the information was out. A large, injured animal would not go unseen in Tucson's suburban streets, or so he liked to hope.

It didn't make sense, it had to be premeditated—but animals don't really *do* that. There were cases where modern science gawked at animal intelligence displaying premeditation, but this felt...on another level. Almost human.

He pressed his forehead to the wheel once stopped at a light. He couldn't be thinking these things. He shouldn't be. Lieu was right to force him off, hell he had wanted off from the start—but he wished he would stop proving her right with these insane theories blooming from prejudice and grief. Vel wanted reason, because from reason he might find justice.

Plus, over and over and over again, *it did not make sense.*

The car behind him laid on the horn and he jolted up. Sheepishness overcame him and he tried to numb his thoughts for the rest of the drive home.

Once there, he noticed a smear on the wheel. It was sauce from the gorditas he had failed to catch. He stared.

Why did the fourth girl have car grease on her hands? Wasn't it just as strange for her to leave her own car if it didn't need mechanical repairs? Using the corner of his shirt to wipe off, he reached for the file in the front seat and pulled out Lieu's scribbled notes. It would've been better for him, personally, if the file was complete like the others; name, occupation, vestiges of the life she had had eking through to ground him through the process. Whatever he had been going through, her loved ones were surely sharing in that. Vel frowned, and resorted to the rest. All had gone missing relatively late in the evening or at night. Runs to the store before it closed resulted in never returning, their cars found abandoned with no sign of trouble. He could only assume that Jane Doe—bless her name, whenever he'd learn it—had much the same happen to her.

Stopping in the middle of the road late at night to work on a car engine that wasn't even hers? It didn't seem right. Vel scrunched his face closed and sighed once, twice, then muffled a frustrated howl into the files. This was the first time he wished it, but god damn it, he *wished* Lieu had been wrong about him.

3

It was a bad idea, but he convinced himself that he had to do it. In his *head* this was better because if he met Shoua at her workplace then nothing weird could happen. Things could not spiral out of control like last time. But, of course, the second her eyes locked to him when he stepped into the bar he knew he had fucked up. Again. Her hackles had raised with the tension and she started wiping the bar down twice as hard as before.

Hell on earth. He wanted to say that it wasn't what she thought, but the bar wasn't exactly empty. Plus, for as careless as he had been there still needed to be *some* semblance of decorum for his work. It wasn't often that his smile felt awkward, but it did as he tried to casually slide onto the barstool. Shoua's shoulders raised and fell with a breath of preparation before she greeted him.

"Vel." her voice held apprehension behind heated stoicism. He wouldn't quite call it professionalism; there was no denying she was *furious* to see him. He shrank as much as his long body would allow.

"I have a question."

For a half-second her lip curled, "*Do* you now."

"Nothing personal," he was quick to explain, "Just... professional. But um, sensitive."

Shoua tightened her jaw, "Are you here to drink?"

He shrugged, "I guess I could take one."

"*One*," she agreed, "That's all you'll get."

"I haven't pre-gamed," he protested, furrowing his brow. He didn't want to get drunk either, but he felt a vague insult from her implications. Still she grabbed a beer glass for him.

"Pilsner?"

"Sure."

"Actually," she tersely corrected herself, "It's been hot. Weiss."

Vel felt himself give a measly smile. It might've just been her at work, but he still understood it as the smallest, tiniest, microscopic bit of care in her correction. She set the pint down hard and he slowly pulled it toward him. In the...Before Laura died, he could see himself complimenting the 'nice head' she had given. An eye roll from Shoua, Laura's elbow in his ribs followed by her sharp laughter and enthusiastic follow-up: *Mine too, Shoua!* Then Shoua's smile would turn sweet, say that it was her pleasure—only for her. It was about as sing-song as Shoua ever got. He missed that. Missed being able to bring that out, because he was never able to do it alone.

"So?" Shoua made direct eye contact, glaring, "What's this question about?"

Vel glanced around the bar to not only take in how many patrons there were (about five including him, it was still relatively early) but to find the television broadcasting the evening news. He stared at it long enough that Shoua got the hint, and when she became stuck there he raised his glass and sipped slowly, watching her. Information about the newest body found was being relayed. The images did not need to be graphic to strike her as it struck him. Once again her shoulders rose and fell, but with a little more shake to them.

"Really, Vel?" she asked quietly.

"Nothing bad. I just need to check something."

She swallowed, fixated on the news. Finally she tore herself away, refusing to look at him again, "My break's in an hour. Let me know if you need any food." He did not swallow his beer in time to respond before she had pulled herself as far away from him as she could.

He looked back to the TV. It was bad for him, he shouldn't have done it, but he had to. Something in him made it so that he had to. The girl's name was Diana Berkeley. Freshly married, university graduate (as he figured), had recently started a stable career—the details turned to mud as he sank in them. *They* hadn't been married but they had been living together in a house she mostly bought with her stable career. People considered them married anyway, even if—upon her death—he learned that Arizona had no cohabitation laws. He had to deal with that at some point, though Laura's family had been gracious enough to not raise questions as to who the house belonged to now. It was too early for Diana to have written a will. Too early for Laura to have a will written either.

Vel sank, pushing the beer forward to make room for his forehead. He clutched the glass, its cool temperature the only thing keeping him there in the moment. Background noise filled in, and he was suddenly glad he couldn't hear the news broadcast. The Diamondbacks game was loudly being played on the one TV that did have sound. Shoua clinked glasses behind the bar as she washed and put them away. Three of the other patrons were at a table, older men chattering about things that were mostly benign but sometimes turned sour to Vel's ears. Speculations, declarations, hemming and hawing over the recent string of crimes. It was news enough, Tucson was a locked-doors city more for property loss than violence. But their speculations swirled in his head and made him sink against the bar harder. Must've been the cartel. Must've been jealous boyfriends. Must've been *a beast, a huge feral coyote, something with sharp fangs and sharper claws that ripped her from her car and—*

Shoua's boss wandered to and from the back, conversing lightly with her when he did. She replied as though Vel wasn't slumped on the bar with a half-drunk glass of beer. Hell, he didn't hear her mention him at all. But at least it tore him from his spiral. At some point, something wicker pushed against his arm. Glancing up through his ragged hair revealed an order of chicken tenders and some botched mozzarella sticks. The pit that had made a home of his stomach growled, both hungry and sick. Guilt made it so much worse. Showing up here was him trying to be responsible, instead he was now being pity-fed by Shoua. He pressed his fingers to the edge of the wicker, tempted to push it back until it fell on the other side of the bar. His arm was long enough to do so. But as much as he loved being petty around her, he had caused enough damage already. Like a dejected kid, he picked at the food. Cheese first, otherwise it'd actually taste as gross as his stomach was trying to tell him it was.

Shoua continued to not look at him, and he didn't ask. Eventually he picked the basket clean and returned to his depressing cocoon.

There had been a patron to his left since he arrived. He was larger than him in width, and though that wasn't hard Vel estimated that he could stand two of himself comfortably within this patron's waistline with room to spare. The size came with ruggedness and grim silence, and he bothered neither Vel nor Shoua despite his definite eye on the situation. Vel guessed him to be a regular, because Shoua moved comfortably in front of him. The occasional word between them was devoid of customer service cordiality, which further cemented Vel's assumption. Shoua could be closer to herself around this patron that didn't ask much of her nor wished to receive bullshit cheer in return.

The same could not be said of the patrons that arrived some time after Vel had finished his beer. (The glass was still in his hand, presumably because Shoua wasn't about to pry the makeshift security blanket away.) Her voice raised in pitch, asking what she could do for them. They slid into the seats on Vel's other side, chatting with each other as Shoua served their drinks. He peeked from his elbow. College students, most likely; either they already lived in town or they were here for the summer term. Certainly they didn't have too much on their plate to hit the bar in the middle of the week.

He listened to them, blindly people-watching. Inane banter. Self-confident affirmations. Real boys-will-be-boys attitudes. It charmed him in a fascinating way, like looking at bugs in a jar—something so common a child could capture it but so alien when observed closely. They paid him no mind and he quite preferred that in his current state.

"Hey, when do you get off?" the kid closest to him asked Shoua, and his voice hit Vel in the back of the neck. Listen. Listen, he *understood* that this was Shoua's job, and that she more than likely had had her fair share of creeps, weirdos, or just maladjusted men hitting on her. She was small and stout, her ripped black clothes and goth aesthetic hardening her soft edges as a warning sign. She knew how to deal with them, and she did—firstly by humoring their question with the dullest tone Vel could imagine.

"Late."

"How late? We'll be bar-hopping for a while."

"Late-late."

The regular to his left shifted in his seat. The movement was small but to Vel's sense unmissable; he was listening just as hard as Vel was.

"What's your name?" tried the other one.

"I'll write it down to see if you pronounce it right." Shoua took a receipt already poked through and scribbled messily on it. To Vel's dismay, the college kids did not seem deterred. If anything their chests puffed up.

"Show-a. It's Japanese. Guess we're picking you up after you're off, huh?"

Utterly humorless, Shoua crumpled the receipt and lightly responded, "Wrong. No second guesses."

Their puffed chests turned to ruffled feathers and they protested—in part as if they found this all to be a joke. Vel had seen the like before. If the situation was a joke, then no weight was put on the seriousness of the rejection. Suddenly Shoua was needled with questions, from how to pronounce her name to where she was from—*was she an island girl? Chinese? Korean? How about a last name?* The two boys were triangulating her position, and though she was ignoring them the annoyance in Vel's neck had mulled to anger.

"What part of *no second guesses* don't you understand? Fuck off." Vel grunted. He had only raised his head enough for them to see that he was glaring at them. Of course, they had the gall to look offended as though he had stepped on their turf.

"Stick to yourself over there. I'm sure she's real impressed by how drunk you are when it isn't even eight." the one further from him shot. Closer to him the kid narrowed his eyes like he was analyzing a situation that did not need any analysis. He raised his hand from the counter to quell his friend.

"Hey man, we're just trying to get to know her. No need to get so upset."

"You're annoying me." Vel shot back.

"Do you own the bar? This is a public space." the further, much more aggressive kid spat. The calmer of the two turned back to Shoua.

"Need help removing him?"

Shoua did not look up, but her voice was firm and unmovable, "He's fine."

"Is he your boyfriend?"

Vel flicked his eyes to Shoua just in time to catch the tension form in her jaw, "No."

"Then there's no need for him to get so defensive. We were just talking."

Shoua shifted herself closer to Vel, making it look like as smooth as if it was her workflow. Still she didn't look up from the glasses she was putting away, "He said you were annoying him. It's a free country."

"Well," the aggressive one exclaimed, "It's free for us too! Free for us to ask anything—*do* you have a boyfriend?"

The tension in her jaw tightened and there was an unmissable pause. No matter what her answer was, the pause said enough. Lying would only make it worse, so Shoua simply answered with a hardened, "No. And I'm not looking. Thanks."

The calmer one had all but turned from Vel, "Ah, we weren't looking either. It wouldn't work out with the three of us—this guy gets jealous easily!" he elbowed his friend in the side. Their laughter was rough and grating in Vel's ears.

They returned to the topic of her name, at first badgering her for the pronunciation before trying to figure it out for themselves. Vel's ears were then mistreated to a cavalcade of horrific sounds, from *Shwa* to *Shower* to *Shao-a*, all wrong, all more and more ridiculous as time went on. It became a game to them, inventing new and terrible ways to say the letters of her name with their gazes fixed to her to gauge any reaction. By the time they started replacing her name at all with bastard phrases and lame jokes Vel snapped. He snatched the arm of the kid closest to him and snarled.

"Shut. The fuck. *Up!*"

The tone shifted in an instant. Both college kids sat up straight as though they could intimidate him. The threat was in their eyes, they were ready to fight—or they believed they were. Realizing that, Vel also sat up straight and towered over them from just the barstool. Most parts of him were gangly and bony, like his body could clack like a marionette if shaken hard enough. But he had the chest of a swimmer, and though it made his proportions awkward the breadth of his shoulders always caught people off guard. Vel spent most of his adult life in a slouch, curled to avoid the tops of doors and fit on beds— there was no indication of strength in his wiry body unless he straightened and tensed.

What's more, whatever threat the kids thought was in their eyes, Vel knew his burned hotter. He was not a brawler, but nor was he in the headspace to back down *at all*. It didn't matter that it came from a spiraling depression, the threat that he *would not quit* was something that a smarter person wouldn't tangle with.

That and, he did catch the kids' eyes glance behind him. Their resolve hesitated, then shrank. Indignant, they nursed their drinks in beaten silence and left without a tip.

When they did, both Vel and the regular to his left turned back to the bar. Shoua was quiet for a moment. Then Vel got the lecture.

"They were likely harmless."

"They *are* harmless until they're not." Vel shot back, furious that she would even say such a thing.

"They were going to bar-hop and forget about me at the next pretty girl they saw. It happens all the time, Vel. And they were never going to remember my name."

"Driving cars is harmless until it's not, too, you know,"

"Vel," she pinched the bridge of her nose, "I'm *fine*. This is my job. You don't need to protect me."

That struck him just as indignant as the kids who left. This wasn't *about* protecting her—perish that goddamn thought! Shoua was too prideful to accept his help anyway, so what was she getting at in the first place?! "Well, they *were* annoying the shit out of me, and this *is* a free country. You said it yourself."

"I'd rather not stop a fight on my shift, you know."

"*I'd* rather—," he stopped. Dead stopped. He was on the verge of saying shit he didn't even want to hear. Shoua stopped too and stared at him, calculating. Heat flushed his face, frustration and fear collapsing in on each other. The words stayed in his mouth, but though he tried not to think them they rattled him anyway.

He'd rather not have another funeral so soon—the same words she said to him the night before.

Shoua sighed. Not in frustration, but in a release of tension and pity that he was starting to become so, so, so goddamn sick of being directed at him. She glanced at the clock.

"Break's in ten."

That was his cue. Vel sullenly pushed the empty beer glass towards her and slunk off the stool. His hand went to his pocket, fishing out a cigarette. Naturally, he needed one suddenly and badly. As he approached the door to leave, he heard Shoua thank the regular. She was met with a gruff, charmingly dismissive grunt.

She would've been fine.

Once again he stepped into the evening desert air away from her, feeling pathetic and foolish and stupid. Vel circled to the back door, lighting the cig and drawing in quick to jumpstart the nicotine. The next draws were purposefully long as he tried to force himself to calm down with the smoke. *Idiot*, Lieu's voice accused him.

It felt a bit wrong and a bit hurtful that what he had done fell in the realm of idiocy. He could see himself interfering even on a good day—but maybe with more grace and tact. Maybe that was wishful thinking—no, it was definitely depressed thinking.

But he'd been through that before. Vel went by Vel for sake of ease. English speakers who weren't used to Spanish didn't just swap the N and M of his first name on paper. Even though he didn't qualify himself as a Spanish speaker it felt hollow to keep correcting people. Some called him Geronimo if it was easier, but he never liked the sound of that. Sometimes he desperately made them settle for Jerome. Vel, however, he could live with Vel. He liked Vel. It fit just right. It didn't quite sound Spanish but didn't sound English either. Kind of weird, kind of in the middle, call him Vel. It was easy and by this point he responded to that quicker than any other amalgamation of his name.

Laura called him Vel, though that wasn't the origin of his name. She called him Vel in public, when she needed his opinion in the grocery store. At home she called him Vel but in a softer way, as though she was upholding a special secret. Maybe she was—it wasn't long after they had started making love that she insisted on calling him something else, something different, something like Jeró. It sighed easily out of her even if the accent was never quite as sharp. It surprised him how much he liked it. Of course, she wasn't the only one. His tía called him that unless she was mad at him. But Laura said it in her own English-speaking unique way.

Then there was Momo, but only his mother called him that. No one else was allowed to, and to keep it that way he never shared that with anyone. Not even Laura.

It was an odd-fitting thought. Maybe it hurt, maybe it was just strange to realize. Momo existed entirely outside of Laura, and because it rested purely in his memory and nowhere else Momo existed after Laura too.

Weird. Strange.

He was used to the weird and strange, though.

Shoua stepped out with a Red Bull in her hand. Vel gave a wave with the little cigarette he had left and kept a respectable distance from her.

"Hey, Boots," he paused, "Sorry about that."

"It's fine, Vel." she sounded like she meant it, and the tiredness was just a byproduct of having to be at work at all, "It's...just been a lot to handle all at once."

He nodded, for once feeling in unison with where she felt.

"So," her voice turned curt, "This 'not personal, professional but *definitely* sensitive question' you have."

And just like that, the unison crumbled to dust. Vel awkwardly cleared his throat and tried to think of how to word what he was going for.

"Uh," he croaked, and under the scrutiny of Shoua's unimpressed gaze the croaking felt all the more damning, "Yeah. Okay. So if you were driving alone and you came across someone on the side of the road needing help, would you stop to help them?"

Shoua mused for a moment, "What kind of help?"

"Car trouble. Hood up and everything."

She frowned, "No." Definitely not, then.

Vel frowned but for a different reason, "Not even if it was me?"

She answered without hesitation, "I think I'd run you over first."

"First—so *after* you'd help me?"

"Only so I wouldn't get implicated." Shoua said dryly. Vel smiled. It was small compared to his usual easygoing smiles, but no matter how short it had been this was the most normal conversation he'd had in a month. He basked in it, however brief it was.

"Why are you asking?" Shoua said, not exactly cutting the moment short but forcing him to move forward.

"Just checking a hunch," he answered, "So it's definitely weird for a girl to do that?"

"I'd say so," she said after a swig of Red Bull, "It's not exactly smart."

"But you would if you knew the person."

"Tough call if I could recognize someone that fast."

Vel bent over to meet her eyes from afar, "Do you need glasses?"

Shoua snarled, "Don't you keep your eyes on the road?!"

"No. I'm Mexican."

Shoua pressed the can to her forehead hard enough to leave a mark and muttered curses to herself before spitting, "And I'm

Asian, what of it?"

"No, you're Hmong."

"How is that different?!"

He shrugged, petulant. Shoua downed half the Red Bull in one go.

"Wait, I got it," he said suddenly, "I hang my shit from the rearview, you hang shit from the wiper switch."

"Goddammit Vel," she muttered, "Don't you have anything better to do? What's the question for?"

"Ah," his voice dropped to a more serious tone, "Sorry. I don't know yet and I can't tell you."

"It's that serious...," she said it more like a statement than a question, and shook her head, "You could've texted me this."

He was quiet for a moment, "I guess."

She was quiet in turn, anxiously upset, "Vel—,"

"Not like that," he was quick to defend himself, "I...I do need to get out. Y'know. I just thought that this would be—less weird."

"Showing up at my work unannounced saying you have a sensitive question to ask me after—," she did not finish the words before moving on, "—is not weird to you?"

"Less weird," he corrected lamely, "Not *not* weird."

She sighed, but it was hard to argue. Vel snuffed out the cigarette under his boot.

"It's uh, at least I can say it's important enough that I needed a pretty quick answer." There. That worked. Shoua nodded, shrugged, nodded again.

Muffled sounds of the bar, busier than before, with other nightlife surrounding them cushioned their relative silence. Shoua checked her phone. Vel looked up at the sparse stars he could see this far in the city. It wasn't exactly comfortable, but both of them had the freedom to leave and didn't.

"Air's thick tonight." Vel commented after a while. Shoua absently hummed in agreement.

"Monsoon starts soon—*fuck*," she cussed and Vel immediately knew why. Her apartment, one of the few buildings with basements in the city, was situated right on the edge of a common flood plain. More than once, in fact about every year since she moved in, the apartment would flood to her knees. Sometimes higher. Complaints to the landlord were met with half-hearted attempts to fix it and dumbass notices that they couldn't do much with her actively living there. The rent was cheap, but somehow not cheap enough to cover the yearly flooding she had now become used to. The building itself was a mistake. Shoua was just waiting for the damage to take the building as a whole so she would have an excuse and leverage to sue the shit out of the landlord for forcing her to live there. For the time being, her hands were too occupied between work and selling her paintings to make ends meet.

Vel was often the one she would call for help when the flooding got too severe. She needed stepladders to reach the top shelves where he only needed to reach a little to put her stuff above the water line. Worst come to worst, which did happen, she'd put boxes of her most precious things in her car and drive them to his and Laura's place. Since buying the house, sometimes boxes of Shoua's things would stay until the monsoons stopped for the year.

Now, of course, that was made awkward—especially so since she no longer had a partner to fall back on to help her. Shoua hid her face in her hands.

"Vel, could you—,"

"Yeah. Sure. Don't worry about it."

She was silent for a long time before giving a gutted and mortified, "...Thanks."

"'Course," he assured her, feeling morose that he had to. That it was made weird, that *he* had made it weird. For once he wished weird stuff would stop following him, just so things could be *normally* weird again. Shoua looked rattled as she finished off the Red Bull.

"Hey, Shoua," Vel said gently, "How are you holding up?"

She scrunched, "Better than you."

"That's a low bar," he parried, "You said it was a lot to handle at once."

"I was talking about work," she said defensively. Vel was undeterred and she scowled, "It's—,"

Something caught in her throat. The scowl wavered, fell, and Shoua's face became nervous stone as she stared down the alleyway. There was nothing in particular that she was looking at; just so long as she wasn't looking at him. Her gaze was often hard and piercing, but his eyes—blue-green against copper brown skin—had their own unique way of piercing. Usually she avoided his gaze as punishment. Now, though, she was avoiding him in order to avoid being read. That in it of itself told him much.

For half a minute he thought she was going to talk. Words rolled in her mouth like she was searching for the right ones to say, but then she ducked her head.

"Sorry. Gotta clock back in."

Vel blinked as she opened the back door, "It's only been twenty minutes—Boots, *Shoua*,"

The door slammed shut. Vel stared at it, spurred halfway to action far too late. Or perhaps, he wouldn't have grabbed her even if his life depended on it—it wouldn't have helped.

He scratched his prickly chin and debated going back inside the bar. Not to talk to her. Just to be there. Hang out. Pretend it was normal to be there.

But it wasn't. Shoua would, intentionally or not, remind him that it wasn't. Vel rubbed his eyes and sighed.

As he drove home he thought about passing cars on the side of the road. Shoua had confirmed his gut feeling. Even he would hesitate stopping for a car in trouble, especially when it was this dark outside. But of course, if he knew them, he would stop without hesitation. In broad daylight that could even cause an accident.

At night, no one would likely be around to notice.

Vel did not want to give a name to the silence Lieu punished him with on the phone, so he didn't. Regardless, she called him back later with the pertinent information. Diana Berkeley wasn't a mechanic, but wasn't exactly dumb with cars either. Knowledgeable enough to get by, or so described by her remaining loved ones. That narrowed down explanations to his hunch that she had stopped at the side of the road to help someone. Likely someone she knew.

Of course he didn't know who, but he passed the deduction along in the hopes that it would be useful. It wasn't what they paid him for, but Lieu graciously didn't turn down a grounded idea.

Pictures were starting to circulate of Diana, lots of them right next to her husband. His skin was about the same shade as Vel's, though he was built more like a construction worker—thick and reliable, not gangly and weird. Further details of Diana's life washed over him, details that he tried to look at as an investigator but hit deeper and deeper the more he dwelled in the case file.

Everything reminded him of Laura, and Diana's husband looking similar enough to him (so to speak) triggered that in spades. Lieu's silence was damning for a reason. He shut the case file and slid it away from him on the coffee table. Crumpled up napkins, a plate from his dinner, and a half-drunk glass of water served as litter around the file. Vel flopped back on the couch. He slowly stretched his legs until they pushed the coffee table askew. The TV flickered, but he was simply keeping it on for company and didn't know what show was on.

It was a coincidence that Laura was murdered in perfect lock-step with the timing of the other murders, anyone would tell him that. But Laura loved coincidences. That thought snagged on his brain like a bur that couldn't be brushed off. It didn't nag like thoughts could when something was wrong but unseen. This felt obsessive and projected. Even he couldn't justify the roads his mind was taking.

Magic, or whatever it was he learned from his mother, shifted nebulously in the world. There weren't rules like the wizards his friend wrote for their tabletop sessions. It was more personal and spiritual than that. The simplest way Vel had ever found to put it was that whatever was brought to it was what he got out of magic. Some people cast spells or held rituals as many in the witchcraft community did, though Vel wasn't a part of that. Some people prayed; Vel had spent enough years under his nun tía's roof that it was both habit and disdainful to pray. Lots of things he did started and ended with hope and belief. A little bit of witchcraft, a little bit of Catholicism, a little bit of "fuck it" because he knew belief was out there even if he had to create it himself. That landed him no real community, but it was handy in a pinch as a private investigator.

If it was a skill or an inherited trait, he couldn't say. Everyone looked at the world differently, and Vel felt that the strongest when he tried to figure out a definition for what made magic *magic*. Maybe the pink-striped stone that he bound with leather cord, wooden beads, and a mouse's rib never gave Laura the good luck he had intended it to give. Maybe his mother's eyes would never decay and he was, in fact, not crazy for keeping them as a deeply personal reliquary.

All that to say, when Vel's logic led him down a path, following it could have dire consequences. There was magic in coincidence purely because it was coincidence. Reading into it led Laura to him, but it could also lead him to madness.

Her body, wrapped around a cactus, blue eyes gray with glaze, skin ashen against the orange sand and browning blood. It was a creature. Not an axe. Not a person. What creature? No one knew. It was coincidental only if he convinced himself it was. Same way Diana and her husband shared Laura and his skin tones.

Vel tipped his head back and rubbed his face. Whatever time it was, it was late enough to sleep. He determined this because he did not want to think anymore. Everything was left on the coffee table as it was overnight.

* * *

The last time he had stepped foot in the police station was to claim Laura's personal things. Whether or not they'd stay with him or go to her parents or the thrift store had yet to be determined. One thing he knew he had to keep was the rock he had bound for her. It was given as a simple charm, similar to a worry stone (and he had already rubbed the harder edges soft so as not to cut through either the leather cords nor her skin). Laura had strung it to a necklace. She had learned over

44

the years not to ask if anything about it had a direct symbolic meaning, because from Vel the answer was often no, or at least not a consistent one. For this pendant, the rock's colors reminded him of her. The leather was the binding agent, the beads were splashes of contrasting color, and the mouse rib was for dexterous escape from danger.

The rib was the only thing he had taken from the remains he had found. That was his rule; there was never a need to take the whole body, it was greedy and deprived both land and spirit from the respect it deserved. It was rare to find a mouse skeleton and so exposed—usually mice wound up in predator or scavenger dung. Trying to figure out how this one had died and been picked clean enough for the bones to be dry but careful enough to be within the same area of each other—it was a rarity. Or perhaps coincidence. So he could say that the mouse rib was for escape from danger, but in reality how he happened upon it made him think of her too.

He cared enough to make it, and that was enough for her, and that was the magic inherent in it. Holding it after her death was bittersweet. It's not like he had made the charm for a specific purpose, but he had made it with a hope and a kiss and now it would never grace her chest again. Vel was only human, and he didn't consider himself a witch, but things sometimes worked.

Sometimes they didn't.

That's how it stayed fair. (It didn't feel fair.)

If he had been in any right mind, he would've found the police's investigation at the time disappointing. It was too bizarre to rule it as a simple, tragic killing, but it's not like Vel had any explanations for how it could've been anything but that. Even if he was sobered up from grief he'd be having a hard time. He distanced himself like he was supposed to, like Lieu told him to.

So of course, her eyes narrowed when she saw him at the front. Thus followed their usual ritual, she'd lead him through the back to which many officers would perk their head up at the tall lanky mess snaking behind the lieutenant. Blithely he wondered if any rumors had started about them, but Lieu had a husband and there were times when that seemed like a miracle. Her two kids likely wouldn't agree, but Vel judged that purely by the distance they had put between their mother and their lives.

"On the case or off?" she asked with the tone of a very disappointed boss.

"On. Off. Unofficially on, officially off?"

Lieu sighed, "I don't think we require your services on this one."

"Still doing detective work on my end," Vel lightly protested and leaned back in the chair across from her desk. It was normal for him to do so, but the action felt strained in the moment.

"Unofficially. Of the highest order." Lieu said flatly.

Vel shrugged. He wasn't hurting anyone, "I had a hunch and asked a friend a question and fed the information to you. Two brains are better than one."

"Too many cooks—,"

"—is a potluck."

"Vel," Lieu turned her office chair to sit in it, and his relaxed pose seemed all the more inappropriate. Her tone was off in that it was soft. He had heard it once before this month of hell, and he didn't like it. He didn't like Lieu feeling this sort of way about him as much as he didn't like Shoua's unprompted kindness, "Being off the case is not just about compromising the investigation."

"I haven't *done* anything yet," the protest was not light this time.

"Yet." she didn't say it definitively, but her usually direct gaze was to the side, as if musing on the possibility, "It's more...,"

Vel waited.

"More...,"

He leaned forward in the chair.

"...Stop that."

"More what?" he prompted, turning his ear to her.

"I am...concerned. That this case is going to hurt you."

"Sorry, didn't catch that," he brought a hand up to his ear, "Again?"

"Vel," she said firmly, "I am being serious."

"Yeah it's awesome, you look like you swallowed a lime."

"*Velasquez.*"

That drained the humor and he sat back in the chair, properly, with his own eyes narrowed.

"I can't involve you with any new information or developments. You must understand. I'll give you pay for the work you've done, but I mean it—you're done here."

He sat with that for a moment. Lieu had a way of speaking like a hammer. Or an anvil falling from the sky. Several times he opened his dry mouth to try and say something in response, only to close it and think more. Lieu was struggling to maintain gentleness—dropping the anvil from seven feet up instead of thirty—but it was clear that she was firm in this decision and it hadn't been hard for her to make.

"This doesn't mean total termination. But. Just. Stay out of this one. For your sake."

"...What if I solve it on my own?"

Her brow knitted in bewildered frustration, "With what, Vel? She was murdered in a truck bed that we'll *probably* find *somewhere* in Tucson? It's barely anything."

"But, she,"

"She *what?*"

Vel looked to the side. She had a husband that looked like him. Vel could imagine exactly what he was feeling.

"You help investigations," Lieu tried, "Maybe even this one. But I have to cut you off. How many more times do I have to tell you?"

"Good thing I didn't bring the file," he muttered, "You woulda taken that too, huh?" Not that it was in the best of hands right now, but Lieu didn't need to know that if she couldn't already sniff that out.

"I should." Lieu dropped another anvil, "I am thinking about it. Don't call for this case again, Vel."

He stood up.

"And take care." she finished quick before he opened the door.

Vel shrugged, "Say hi to your kids for me, Lieu."

It stung him even as he said it. Lieu was right and didn't deserve such a low blow—not from him, anyway. But he felt a snarl on the edges of his mouth as he ducked back out through the station, the same pairs of eyes on him but feeling far more eagerly hungry for gossip than before.

He kept fucking showing up where he didn't belong, or in places he half-belonged but got shooed out of. Wringing his hands on the steering wheel, Vel felt his insides gnash and snarl and whimper at him for his actions. Actions that may not have been stupid from a certain point of view, but that made him *feel* stupid.

But hey. His mother jumped the border. His tía rejected everything his mother raised him with and threw almost all of her things away (if he didn't save them first). He refused to go to church after a certain point. His eyes were blue-green and his skin was brown. He ticked 'mixed/other' on the census. It was in his blood to *unbelong* somewhere. It just fucking sucked that without Laura those somewheres were narrowing and narrowing, and his body was tall and gangly and there were only so many times he could fold himself over to fit in the space.

Because *both* Lieu and Shoua were right and of all the things he did believe he wished he didn't believe that.

5

A few days came and went. Nights were his most active. As it was, it was incredibly hard to measure how many full days were passing him by when every time he glanced out the window it was dark. Still. There was something peaceful in the solitary depression. Vel didn't feel much like talking to people after Lieu's confrontation anyway.

Part of him heard the rain on his roof, though he wasn't actively paying attention. It made sense for mid-summer. Someone recently had mentioned to him that the monsoon rains were going to start. That felt more important than he was understanding in the moment, but he couldn't quite remember why. He tucked into another single-serve frozen pizza dinner. He knew how to cook, and because he knew how to cook the pizza felt flat and soggy in his mouth. The flavors were sucked away by preservatives and the cheese was stiffly not fresh. Vel's stomach hated it. But it was food. In fact it was the only food that kept him full because it grossed him out so much he wouldn't go back for seconds. Or thirds. Or fourths. That's what his usual descriptor of having a trash can for a stomach meant, instead of stuffing it with frozen food that was more expensive than just buying fresh ingredients.

He was tired, his soul was sick, the frozen pizza did not

help but it was the only thing he could do. If he bought fresh ingredients they would either turn to ash in his mouth or in his fridge. Whichever managed to happen first.

The doorbell rang frantically and he shoved the last bit of crust in his mouth and forced a swallow. Pizza sauce on his thumb was better suited to where he wiped them on his jeans. He opened the door.

Shoua stood there wide-eyed with adrenaline and hefting two stacked boxes that crested over the top of her head.

"Sorry—*sorry* they're early!"

They—what? Oh, the rains, Shoua's apartment, *shit*. Vel pulled the top box off and quickly retreated to the living room with Shoua in tow. Once they were set on the couch he had the wherewithal to grab his black denim jacket before following her. She was speaking fast and he was grateful for it because his brain had to jog to keep up and in that jogging it was occupied.

"Two more in the car but there's more in the apartment— Shit, if it's already this bad,"

The rain pelted him the second he stepped outside. By the time he reached her small SUV in the driveway he was already flipping his wet hair back to keep it out of his eyes. Vel hung his arms low so she could pile both boxes into them. Pinning them in place with his chin, he precariously balanced on one arm for a moment before throwing the jacket over the top to protect them from the rain. Shoua got back into her car while Vel put them inside and locked the door. With rain pouring this hard already, his old sedan was asking to sail the flash flood down into Mexico.

Shoua breathed curses. Her windshield wipers were already at the highest speeds. Vel gave a sidelong glance to the red string hanging from the wiper switch. He liked taking special notice of such things. Part of him wanted to ask what it meant to her, but the urgency was ramping and he had to take a rain check on that question.

"You think it's gonna hit the old water line on the wall?" he asked. Shoua's voice hissed through her teeth.

"Maybe—I don't know. This is already—," she paused after backing out and bent forward to look up at the dark sky, "Don't think we should be driving."

Vel pitched forward too but with a decidedly sharper curve in his back, "Too late to turn back?"

"Yes, I—," Shoua snapped, "There's things I can't lose and I wasn't looking when I packed most of the boxes, the water started leaking by the time I left!"

She sped forward, throwing Vel back into his seat proper. The headlights did more harm than good with how much the light flickered and reflected off of the rain drops, and the further she drove northside the slicker and brighter the roads became. Shoua's curses got quieter as the rain substituted for her pounding heart.

"That thing gonna protect us?" Vel asked, his own heart picking up the pace.

"What?" Shoua's knuckles were pale as a near-solid spray of water flared on Vel's side.

"The string,"

"I—I don't know, I'm concentrating! It's supposed to help, alright?"

Another spray of water from a puddle that was deeper than it looked and Shoua yelped. Vel's hand ducked into his pocket and back out and Shoua yelped again, *harder*, when he clamped it on the steering wheel.

"*Vel, for fuck's sake!*"

"Yeah yeah yeah yeah, I know, trust me, okay?!"

"Trust *what*, what are you doing?!"

Vel raised his fingers and shook them. The charm he had made Laura flicked back and forth, clacking against the steering wheel before he wrapped it back up into his palm.

"That's—," Shoua breathed.

"It is," he answered quickly without allowing time to dwell on it, "Okay *go*, drive, I'll steer!"

Shoua clamped her mouth shut, sucked in a breath, and pressed the accelerator. For the most part Vel felt her release the wheel, though one hand stayed opposite of his. Now, *what* was he doing? Yeah, he didn't know. He just felt like this was going to help, and if he threw himself wholly into that belief (and if Shoua did too, though he tried not to count on that) then he could make it work.

Vel kept his eyes fixed on the road, his focus informed by the shifting of the pendant between his palm and the wheel. When it moved he moved, and more than once he told Shoua to help him turn entirely left or right.

"Can't believe you haven't moved out yet," Vel said, easing the wheel to the side to avoid a particularly flooded curb.

"I would *love* to, Mr. Eastside!" Shoua exclaimed, "But the rent is cheap enough to afford it by myself!"

"It fuckin' better be! Can't believe you got a basement in the first place."

"How was I supposed to know?!" she snapped, "Basements are normal in the midwest! Shouldn't you be asking why they were renting one out instead?!"

"Probably earning back what it cost to build the goddamn thing," Vel grumbled.

"Well, it's all a waste, and they do shit to seal it properly every year."

"What are they waiting for, the insurance company to declare it an Act of God?"

"*You tell me!*"

"Shit," Vel muttered, "Left on Grant."

"You've gotta be *fucking* kidding me." Shoua still turned with him, furious. They were now headed in the opposite direction. Though Vel would course-correct soon enough the detour down multiple lanes of Grant Road's traffic did nothing to put her at ease.

"Yeah well that's what you get for living near Grant. I'm going hands off for a sec while you maneuver."

Shoua rolled her eyes, "Yes, thank you *so* much."

"You can thank me after we're back at our—my place, with all your stuff." Vel said, rubbing his thumb across the pendant in gratitude. Her knuckles were still white—hell he was having a hard time not death-gripping something himself—but the fact that they could bicker throughout the entire trip was evidence enough that the charm was working.

"Look on the bright side," Vel said as he placed his hand back on the wheel once she had turned off of Grant some blocks down, "After years of being flooded a sinkhole will open up and you can finally class action lawsuit your way to a better apartment."

"Do you have a charm for that?" she snipped, entertaining more of the idea than her tone let on. Vel snorted.

"I don't think you need a disaster one at this point."

"Thank you, vote of confidence accepted." Shoua scowled.

"So polite today," Vel commented, "Lots of thank yous!"

Shoua cursed, cursed, and cursed again as they finally maneuvered to her apartment. Vel winced getting out of her car and splashing into running water. He watched Shoua's shoulders bulge as she yanked her door open in the inch of water on the lowered ground. More cursing. The water was lapping at his toes as he rushed in as quickly as possible without compromising his balance. Shoua wasted no time handing boxes to him from her couch—the same one he had tongued her on far too recently. But there was no time to be awkward, especially since Shoua showed no signs of thinking about it.

Each tower of boxes he threw his jacket on top of, each trip back the water was a little bit higher. The stain on her wall from previous floods barely made it halfway up his shin, and it was eating above his ankles by the time the couch was cleared. Shoua made a double check of the outlets around her apartment and Vel stashed whatever he could on the highest part of her bookshelves. Picking up her stretched and unpainted canvasses, Vel set them high on her bed while she pulled the blankets into a mound on top of it.

"Everything good?" he asked. Shoua twisted her mouth.

"No but it'll have to do." It was a crap job, but they were out of time.

Back in the car Vel grimaced at the squishing sound in his boots as he adjusted in his seat. Shoua took in several meditative breaths, turned the car on, and headed back onto the road. Vel resumed his place on the steering wheel.

"Back the way we came?" Shoua asked.

"Who knows."

It wasn't the same route, and as Vel guided them back he noticed streets that had been fine before glistening in such a way that he couldn't tell if it was just a trick of the headlights or an unfathomable puddle. He swallowed. Cars all around them were going slow, just as nervous as they were.

The pendant jerked hard, biting into his palm. Vel sucked in a breath through his teeth and jerked the wheel just as hard. The SUV veered from the center of the road, skirting the edge of a puddle that sprayed a thick crest of water. Shoua yelled, clamping her hands down and struggling to wrench control from him.

"What the *fuck*, Vel, don't just *drive on the sidewalk!*"

Vel blinked and looked behind them, "That big puddle in the middle of the—shit," He watched as the car following them kept driving straight. Suddenly the headlights dipped, there was a sound lower than the battering rain, and Vel felt his chest clench, "*Shit*, Shoua, pull over!"

Shoua's eyes whipped to the rearview then back to the road, skidding to park too close to a stop sign. Vel scrambled out of the SUV while she jammed the hazard lights on, taking his jacket as an umbrella. When he was clear, Shoua reached for the glove compartment. Vel took what looked useful—a flashlight and a glass breaker—and sprinted to the half-sunk car. Flashing the light into it revealed only one passenger, a woman who flinched from the brightness but frantically hit the windshield for help.

"*Vel!*" Shoua called from behind him as he gingerly tried to toe out the edge of the pool, "I'm calling 911! Don't fall in!"

"Yeah!" he shouted back to confirm he heard, but all his focus was on the car. It had sunk driver's side down, pinning the door shut. The passenger side was more accessible, only it was across a stretch of water that he couldn't be sure of the depth of—or what was underneath. The woman seemed rooted in the driver's seat though he could see the seat belt hang free. Vel frowned. The trunk was pitched in the air, back wheels hanging on what he assumed was the edge of the hole. Vel made hand signals to the driver's wide eyes before skirting around the back.

Carefully, Vel braced his feet behind the wheel and leaned

across the trunk. In the corner of his eye from the street lamps he saw Shoua dart up near his side but on firmer ground. On the phone her voice was pitched higher, not from customer service but from fear. Vel reached, his belly pressed to the trunk, and struck the window as high as he could. It turned into a cloudy mess of spiderwebbed glass, and he grunted in satisfaction and pulled his legs up to kick.

"*Hey!*" he yelled as soon as part of the window dislodged, "Hey, what's your name?"

"Emily!" she shouted back, twisting in the driver's seat once the window was cleared from the frame.

"Emily," he confirmed, shaking out his jacket and laying it across the backseat to cover as much of the sheet of broken glass as he could, "I'm Vel. Can you crawl back here? I'm tall, I can pull you out."

"Um, I don't know,"

"Are you hurt?"

"I hope not," her voice squeaked, but regardless she tried to move. The water was up to her thighs, and she was fighting gravity to push the seat back to give herself more room. Vel leaned forward into the car, bracing himself against the roof.

She was pregnant. Not quite ready to pop, but close enough that with the weight of the water and the awkward angle, she was stuck.

Alright. Vel pulled his legs up and slid in. Shoua shouted in angry concern and ran up to the back end of the car.

"*Are you crazy?!*"

"Emily, don't ask how many times she's said that tonight," Vel said, partially to diffuse the situation, partially to avoid acknowledging the reality in favor of working against the clock. Of course, Shoua was still on the phone, so he was treated to her frantically and angrily recounting what he was doing to the dispatcher. Unwinding the pendant from his palm, he handed it to Emily, "Hold this. For good luck."

She took it gratefully and without question, holding it tight as Vel reached over behind her seat.

"Might need your help, I'm gonna flatten the seat backwards. There's less water resistance and it should create a slope to crawl up. Okay?" Emily nodded and Vel reached back to reposition his jacket, "Shoua, I'm gonna push her up—she's pregnant."

One last recounting to the dispatcher, and Shoua confirmed after hanging up. Vel tried not to make it obvious he was gritting his teeth. The seat came down, Emily pulled her legs up, and he helped inch her along like a worm over the backseat. For the frightening situation, Emily's face was hard-set, her mouth shut and her nostrils flaring to quell any further panic. Vel countered her weight by lifting her legs and pushing until she gripped the lip of the trunk. Shoua helped brace her arms and Vel scrambled back up and out, nicking the side of his hand in the process. With Shoua's lower center of gravity and Vel's reach, they swung Emily free and onto the pavement.

"Wait, wait wait," Vel said and climbed back onto the trunk to grab his jacket. He shook off the glass in the rain while Shoua helped Emily to the sidewalk. Catching up just as they ducked into a bar, Vel let out a whoop of relief.

"That was somethin', huh?" he briefly offered his jacket to Emily, realized it was more soaked than she was, and retracted the offer, "Any scuffs or scratches?"

"Probably a few," Emily admitted, but any fear that had been in her face before was quickly passing to acceptance and tired gratitude. *Very* tired gratitude, she sat herself at a table with a heave of exertion, "I'll just, call my boyfriend and...sit and wait,

I think."

"You sure?" Shoua asked, and Vel tagged in.

"Her car is still working, we could probably drop you off somewhere."

Emily scoffed and laughed, and Vel realized a little too late how cockily dumb that sounded, "No—I think, I don't know, I'd rather wait for things to die down before I get in a car again. But—thanks," Emily handed the pendant back over to him, "Vel and...Shoua, right?"

"Ones and onlys in Tucson. Probably." Vel said, the residual adrenaline fueling the gaudy, cavalier tone.

"Thanks." Emily said, genuine but tired. She gazed out the window, watching cars slowly creep around where hers had fallen, continuing forward with heightened senses of caution. Resting her hand on her belly, she lost herself for a moment before closing her eyes and readjusting her seat, "I'll be fine. You get out of the flood. Thanks again."

Vel stood still for a moment, though he couldn't figure why. It took Shoua's tug at his arm to shake him free, and he trotted after her.

"Alright," Shoua said when they got back to her car, "You steer."

"What, you didn't believe it before now?"

"Not like...that."

"Damn," Vel said, re-wrapping the pendant into the palm of his hand, "Good thing you believe in the red string, then, otherwise who knows what would've happened."

"Can I ask one thing, Vel?"

"Sure."

"No more jokes about sinkholes."

He laughed, "You know what, yeah. Fine."

The rest of the way was monumentally uneventful in comparison. Hell, *because* of the sinkhole, the urgency and panic of getting Shoua's things to safety felt much less of a problem. So much so that unloading boxes from the car went at a leisurely pace. A box Vel was carrying had a curious whiff about it—not exactly a *smell* so much as a *sensation of a smell*, and it confused him as much as it piqued his curiosity. He set the box down on the floor next to the coffee table (thank god Shoua had not mentioned the trash piling on it) and sat on the edge of the couch.

Snooping wasn't exactly on the forefront of his mind, especially not when he had in previous years helped Shoua pack these same boxes. But from everything that had happened, his mind was cottony and muffled. Vel peeled back a flap.

It was haphazard, but lots of photos were tossed at the very top of the box. Vel carefully collected them in their different sizes. Peeking beneath them he recognized some of the stuff—not from Shoua, but from Laura.

Of course, they shared a lot of things over the course of their friendship. They had known each other for about two years before Laura ran into Vel and were thick as thieves. If Laura couldn't find something in their house, she would call Shoua and it would turn up with her. Vel felt his mouth pull into a sad, distant smile.

He looked at the pictures, and that smile wavered in pain. Ones from Laura and Shoua's favorite smoothie joint. Their graduation from the University of Arizona. Then there was a picture he hadn't seen before of Shoua sitting next to Laura on a couch. Laura's leg was propped up and when he turned the photo he realized that it was covered in the same bruises that his bike had given her. Then in the next picture he was there with the two of them, walking downtown before an outdoor music festival. A chuff of breath left his chest that he thought was a laugh but he could've been wrong. More pictures, others. He dropped them back into the box without dwelling too hard (he had already dwelt enough).

There was one last one, folded over. He mindlessly opened it, but Laura wasn't staring back at him. Nor was Shoua. Vel's mind blanked. The photo was mostly black, save for short white scratches that formed a circle around a black center. And within it, there were more white scratches in the shape of a vague jelly bean. With arms.

Vel was shaking. A piece of small, cute notebook paper had been tucked inside the photo. He had to calm down. It wasn't what it looked like. It couldn't be. He flipped the paper over. It was scribbled on with both Laura's wide, bubbly handwriting in blue and Shoua's tighter, sharper handwriting in black. Notes. Ideas. Plans. Dates, times, what to buy, what to say—*how to tell Vel.*

Shoua re-entered the house with the last of the boxes, sighing in satisfaction. Something had left her mouth, words, a question, he didn't know. Whatever it was it stopped mid-syllable when she saw him. The box she was holding fell to the ground, something shattering within it.

"Vel, *don't—!*"

It was too late. Vel looked up at Shoua with tears streaming down his face. Laura's ultrasound trembled in his grasp. It was far, far too late.

6

There was a tense silence battered only by the rain and a distant rumble of thunder. Vel stared at Shoua and she stared back. Her mouth was closed, her eyes were wide—she knew there was no explanation she could give to cover herself.

Every one of Vel's ribs felt cracked at once. The world crunched and suffocated. Dizzy and gasping for air, Vel started making sounds like a wounded dog. Occasionally they sounded like the start to question words, *what, why, how, when*, but they only ever remained as ragged animal noises.

Shoua took a step backward. He could only imagine that he looked the worst a human being could—half-drowned in rainwater, trembling and unfocused and haggard from weeks of frozen dinners. Sobbing. Destroyed.

"...I should go." she muttered.

Vel sprang to his feet before she could turn, "*No!*"

Shoua staggered. Never had she ever heard Vel truly shout, shout so hard his voice cracked on the edges and wheezed on the way back down. The sound was frightening and unpredictable, and as Vel stumbled forward she took more steps back.

"*Don't go!*" he screamed, "*Don't go!*"

Shoua stumbled back into the front hall and he caught himself on the archway into the living room. His knees knocked and his shoulders raised with every panicked breath. Yes, *panicked*, that was the word for it—he was hyperventilating, sobbing, panicking so hard he could barely see straight. And Shoua, despite her boots, was nearly two feet shorter than him.

"*Please stay here!*" he begged, clocking the primal fear in her eyes. Vel swallowed, his saliva cold and his mouth dry. It felt as though his voice was shrieking from within a tumbling vessel, not a body. The words were under his control, but everything else? He didn't know what was going to happen, he couldn't control the shaking of his hands and his forehead blazed hot. Shoua's eyes were rounded in white, and he kept pushing out whatever words he could, "Not like that, I don't want that—I don't *want that*, I just, I don't want to, *I don't want to be alone, but not like that I don't want to be alone Shoua please*—,"

Vel cut himself short. The whites of Shoua's eyes remained as they were. He was scared. He was *terrified*. Something was wrong and he couldn't control his body, everything was crashing and he didn't even have the wherewithal to figure out if he still trusted her or not. All he knew was that he couldn't be alone. If Shoua left...If Shoua left and if the rain closed in around him, alone with pictures of Laura and the child he didn't know she was carrying, he didn't know. He didn't know.

Vel stood in the archway, staring despondent and pleading at Shoua's eyes. Brutal logic cut through the panic. Laura had been pregnant. She had told Shoua. Laura had died and Shoua didn't tell him. He hadn't known. He hadn't known she was pregnant. And Shoua was going to leave him or feared that he was going to make her stay. God forbid, that he was going to hurt her in a fit of despair.

A flash of anger colored the fear. Then the fear overtook it, more anger, more despair—more and more things until Vel, in his entirety, gave up. With another glance at the photo and note in his hand, he felt the heat of his tears rejuvenate and he collapsed, sobbing on the floor.

They had talked about having a kid. Hell, they had talked about it enough that if an accident were to occur they would have no problem calling it a happy one. And the more they talked the more an 'accident' was due to happen. Vel hadn't given it any thought when she died. Surely, surely, both she and he had been spared the pain of losing not just one life but two.

And it came to him again like a flash in the pan—the way she was curled around that cactus. She had known, full well known when she was attacked. Despite the child not even large enough to be called a child yet, her body warped around protecting it as if there was still a chance. As if she still wanted to tell him.

Another glance and he wanted to throw up. Wrenching his gaze away, he hid his eyes in his other hand. Shoua was still standing in the hallway, and the shame of the state of him made him bite his lip as if he could stifle the sobbing.

Shoua stood for a long time. He was full well expecting to hear her skitter out the door—however she could manage that with boots, but he believed she could. The longer she stood the more embarrassed and ashamed he got. He begged her to stay, now in his mind he was begging her to leave.

"It's not...It's not that I kept it from you. It's...Vel, I couldn't. I'm sorry, I couldn't tell you."

One of her heavy steps. Another. But not toward the door. Vel allowed himself to look, although it was hard from the blurring of his vision. Shoua carefully slid the notebook paper out from his shaking grasp.

"The last time I saw her...was to figure out how to tell you. Laura wanted to make it special, so much so that I was the only one who knew. Because she could trust me not to tell," Shoua shrugged, "...I guess I didn't."

Shoua stared at the piece of paper with her chin behind her knees.

"When you called me the next morning because she hadn't made it home...,"

Vel mustered his voice again, raspy and pathetic, "Please stay."

She looked over, and the calculations behind her expression hurt him to see. He swallowed hard. Convincing her that he wasn't asking for sex, or at the very least physical comfort, seemed impossible. Hell, if he was being charitable to the situation, he didn't know *what* he wanted. *Something.* He needed *something.* Couldn't parse what that *something* was. But he was terrified and the night was as dark as the blackness on the ultrasound.

Rubbing his eyes and grimacing in pain, he tried again and winced at his voice's lack of stability, "I'm scared. I'm scared to be alone. *Please.*"

If it softened the calculations on her face, Vel didn't allow himself to see it. He bent over and dug the heels of his palms into his eyes, avoiding whatever answer she was going to give him. He heard her stand up and walk to the door. Painfully he willed himself silent even if the emotions were threatening to burst him at the seams.

Then, the sound of buckles, two heavy thuds, followed soon after by bare feet on the stone tile. Shoua tugged on his arm and he pushed his back against the wall to stand up.

"I don't want to...," he swallowed hard.

"You already made it weird a week ago." Shoua said bluntly, hiding the tension well. Still, there was something gracious about her tone—guilt, perhaps. Immense guilt. He raised the ultrasound to glance at it again and Shoua jerked her gaze away like it would make her sick. He stared at her like that, with the angle of her jaw facing him. She had apologized like there was no apology great enough for it. Vel wondered if she could even ask for forgiveness.

Probably not.

She heaved several deep breaths, though not exactly calming ones. Then she asked, with her own voice cracking, "Are you gonna be okay?"

He rubbed his nose and looked at the jelly bean that had been in Laura's stomach, "I don't know." The sentence ended on a whimper.

Shoua remained like that in front of him, breathing deep with tensed shoulders and staring off and away into the living room.

"You didn't tell anyone?" he asked.

"Of course I didn't," she gruffly snapped, insulted he would suggest the opposite. Then she croaked on unshed tears, "How fucking could I?"

"...So you haven't talked to anyone about it?" Vel paused, "Any of it?"

Shoua didn't answer. Vel stared at her in the resulting stillness.

"Boots...," he reached for her, but she twisted her arm out of reach and weaseled away.

"Don't make it weirder." she chided harshly. Her feet moved quick to get away from him, entering the living room proper. She stopped at the box he had pulled the photos from, but whatever plans she had evaporated as she looked down at it. No doubt the pictures were affecting her just as much as they had him. Vel's heart sank, and he shuffled his leaden feet to

Shoua's side. Slipping the notebook paper out of her hand, he wiped his eyes clear and actually read the ideas. It wasn't easy. He had to wipe his eyes a few more times, and some of his tears had already blotched out some of the words.

"The...ideas were good." he tried, croaking, "The uh...bear. That would become the...It's cute."

Shoua whipped around to look at him, snapping, "Why are *you* trying to make *me* feel better if *you* were the one that didn't want me to leave in the first place?!"

Vel deflated. Not shrank, he wasn't intimidated by Shoua. But nor could he grasp what she was getting at. It's not like he didn't understand—he had already done so many things he regretted in the past week, let alone since Laura's death. Memories of making out with Shoua haunted him, purely because he couldn't remember anything *about* Shoua in the moment. What did her mouth taste like? How did she move? And her body, thicker than his but half his size all the same—what did that feel like under his hand? He didn't know. It was as if it hadn't happened, but it very, *very* much had.

What would Laura say to her? He looked down at the piece of paper. Laura had once described Shoua as a really good guard dog—cutting her off from people that needed to be cut off and standing up for her when no one else would. But, Laura noted in frustration sometimes, Shoua did not extend herself those same courtesies. Rather, she did it in different and much more personal ways. It wasn't any of his business, but it didn't seem like her last boyfriend was much of a winner if he dipped out on her during the stress of putting on a funeral. He swallowed. If Shoua was the guard keeping things at bay and letting emotions glance off her shoulders, then Laura was the emotional stronghold.

"It...makes me feel better," he said mournfully, "To at least try to cheer someone up."

If Shoua scoffed it was covered by her kicking the box aside with her foot. She reached for one of the others on the couch, pulling out her PlayStation.

"Why *you*?" Shoua blurted all of the sudden, and the sinking feeling that Vel had turned into a twisting stab in the heart, "Why did she have to date someone like *you?*"

Horror braced him, rooting him to the spot as Shoua angrily unpacked games and began setting up the console on the TV.

"This isn't *fair*," she growled, "That she died and left *you* behind!" her growl became a shout, slamming the cords into the console.

Vel, heart crumpling in new levels of despair, spoke past his cottony tongue in a low voice, "...Should it have been me instead?"

"*What?*"

"Me instead."

Shoua opened her mouth, glanced over at him, *saw* his expression, then jolted upright and slammed her mouth shut. There was a stinging around his eyes as he stared at her, wasted away instead of feeling the sick, tender betrayal up front.

Vel worried the edge of the ultrasound, "Would you trade me for Laura?"

"*No*," Shoua cut him off, the harshness pitching into the beginnings of panic, "That's not what I—*no*, Vel, I meant, *fuck*, oh my god,"

It's okay. He didn't just make things weird, he *was* weird. Vel understood. Shoua didn't have to say it. God he wanted a cigarette.

"God damn it," her voice cracked, "*No*, I meant—I wish you

were a *jerk*, an asshole, someone I could just leave behind and feel relieved that she's dead because then at least she wouldn't have to spend her life tethered to you. But *no*, no, you're—," Shoua bit her lip, "You're not that."

He *needed* a cigarette. Blinking and looking away he took one out and placed it in his lips, chewing the ends of it with his teeth as he searched for his lighter. It wasn't in his pocket when they left for Shoua's place, so it had to be somewhere in the mess he had made of the living room. Shoua's breaths became more frequent and high-pitched as time went on, frantic to find further explanation. He would almost call it a search for forgiveness but he didn't think Shoua would like it being worded like that. Frankly, he didn't know if there was anything to forgive so much as forget. He'd like to forget everything, this whole night, this week, this month.

"Vel, say something," Shoua shook, weak and afraid, "Say something now, like you always do."

"Huh? Oh," he mumbled past the cigarette, "Sorry."

"What do you mean *sorry*, I—," Shoua stopped herself before her emotions took over again, biting her lip hard and turning away, her foot restlessly stomping the floor. He turned the words she tried to save herself with in his head. In some respects it was too late, the impact no matter the intent ravaging the inside of his heart. On a regular day he'd have a thicker skin. He was also still thinking about the baby.

What would Laura say? Vel couldn't conjure the answer anymore. It was all too jumbled, a memory fading fast. Soon he'd no longer be able to hear her voice, remember her hugs, or find her a familiar face. It would hit him the hardest when one day he'd be cooking something he'd made thousands of times over and thousands more with her. Something about the flavor would be off, and it wouldn't matter how much salt or spice or prayers he'd put into it, the flavor was off and would forever be off.

It had happened with his mother.

Vel pulled his lighter out from between the couch cushions and headed towards the back patio. He didn't turn the light on before sliding the door open and closed behind him. Rain pattered on the overhang like a snare drum, falling in sheets around the porch like makeshift walls. Flick, light, puff, drag, breathe. He stood between the two padded lounge chairs, staring out into the darkness of the rain.

If, perchance, he heard Shoua's SUV start up, he didn't know how to stop her. He'd run out, sure. He couldn't blame her, sure. But it'd be too late. If he finished his cig and stepped back into the house and she was gone, well, the next parts lay mercifully, terrifyingly blank to him.

As it was, halfway through his cigarette the door sheepishly slid open.

"Vel...can I ask you something?"

The grave tone of her voice made him glance back, seeing her small and bordered in the door frame, scared to cross the threshold.

"Yeah," he allowed, turning back to the rain.

"Why did you ask me that question at work the other day?"

"Oh," he said, a little relieved it was just that, "For the current case. I had a hunch and Lieu is too weird of a woman to give me a good answer on that. Plus she thinks I'm making it personal. Plus...y'know. Maybe I am."

The rain continued.

"Don't you...," she sucked in a breath of courage, "Don't you believe I did it?"

He whipped around, "What?"

"I was the last one to see Laura alive. I was the only one that knew she was pregnant," she turned so the door frame dug into her back, "I knew the route she'd take back home. I knew...everything."

Vel stared at her, hardened and stern, "No. You didn't kill her." he turned away.

"How can you be so *sure?*" she demanded weakly, "Did the pendant tell you that too?"

He whipped his stare back at her, again, "Motive?"

Shoua shrugged, "I don't know, take your pick. What does it matter?"

"Tell me how you made it look like an animal and I'd consider it," he said darkly, "But no. You didn't do it."

"On what? Intuition? Your witchcraft or whatever you call it? Vel—,"

"Your car doesn't smell like blood, Boots," he said firmly, "Laura's didn't either. Out here, in the middle of an Arizona summer, it doesn't matter how well you'd scrub that thing. It'd seep in and the heat would only bring it out. And in the time frame you couldn't have dragged her body so far without one. You don't even park under an overhang. No. You didn't kill Laura."

Shoua's eyes dropped, contemplating.

"But," Vel took another long drag of the cigarette, "You did tell me one thing. You think she was murdered, too."

Not killed. Murdered. Shoua looked back up, her gaze harrowed, hardened, sad.

"I mean, yeah. How could I...not?"

Vel watched his breath of smoke twist in the damp air, then backed up and let himself fall into one of the lounge chairs with a sigh. He rubbed his forehead and grimaced.

"I miss her, Boots."

Shoua stepped outside and took the opposite chair. Finally, after everything, she admitted, "Me too."

Vel cussed, dropping the cigarette butt on the patio with a jerk. Grumpily he kissed his singed fingers, then reached down to pick it up and stuff it in the beer can he kept outside. He didn't fall asleep, but certainly he had lost track of the last minute of the cigarette's life. The rain lulled him. Well, the rain and Shoua's quiet presence lulled him.

"Hey, do you have an extra cigarette?" she asked as he flicked ashes into the can.

"You smoke?" he asked, recalling no such smell from her clothes nor apartment.

"Seems like a good time to start." Shoua replied, exhausted.

Vel chuckled, "Yeah, I thought so too."

"You only just started?" she asked. Vel, assured that her interest was superficial, settled back into the chair and groaned.

"No, I think I was...sixteen? Pissed off my tía so I kept doing it. *¡Ay Jeró apestas a caca de burro!*" he paused with a wry smile of old pride, "Didn't even hide it after a point."

"Thought you didn't speak Spanish," Shoua said, a smile returning to her voice if not her face. Any other person but her and he would've taken a strange offense to that, but she was saying it with a deeper knowledge than most. He had never heard her speak Hmong, but Laura had on occasion. It had come up in conversation between them only once, and that conversation was Shoua refusing to 'show it off' at all, with reddened embarrassment that he understood to be shame.

Vel gave a dry chuckle, "Only that Spanish. Anything else went *whoosh*."

Another, softer groan as his ass settled further in the chair. He watched a particular corner of the overhang where the rain gathered in heavy strings, dripping fat and audible on the stone patio above the snare drums.

"After I moved out there was no one to piss off with it, so I smoked less. I met Laura, quit entirely. I thought, man, quitting was easier than they said it would be," Vel gave another chuckle, this time hollow and resigned, "Well."

There was the slightest smirk that flashed across Shoua's face, and though it was only in Vel's peripherals he treasured it. Any normalcy, any hint of happiness, anything to balance out this horrible fucking time. Be it a cigarette or Shoua sitting near him to make sure he didn't do anything truly stupid. Actually, he could go for another cigarette.

Shoua pulled out her phone while he lit up. Vel continued to watch the rain fall, allowing himself to think but not concentrate. (And, of course, to keep better track of his cigarette before it burned him—but he had marks on his long fingers from it happening many times before anyway. No way to truly help it, but he tried.)

She inhaled, shaky and unsettled. Vel glanced over, his head tilted back to rest on the chair.

"What's up?"

Shoua shook her head, then answered, "Um. Looking at Laura's Facebook."

Ah. He took a drag of the cigarette, staring at the overhang in contemplation. Actually, probably, it wasn't such a bad idea. Catharsis had a hard time bubbling up in him on its own, he couldn't imagine how it was for Shoua. Vel tucked the cig in his teeth and pulled out his phone as well.

"I'll join you."

The next however long was spent quietly scrolling through photos and memories. Occasionally a video would crackle from their sub-par phone speakers; Laura's voice, or Shoua's, or Vel's—her laughter, or cries of shock from a prank. One particular video made Vel smile though there was pain in his throat. Laura was hunched over the comal in hyper concentration and hesitation. She was determined *and* afraid of flipping tortillas by hand, trying, yelping, pulling her hand back and shaking it, jumping, shouting in horror as the tortilla slid off the side. He heard his chuckle from the other side of the camera, eagerly patient as he watched the scene unfold. Laura chastised him for laughing, it was scary! Of course, he laughed harder. At least one tortilla ended up a tostada. Another puffed up.

"*You know what that means, right?*" he asked her.

"*What? Is it on there too long? Vel—,*"

"*Means you're gonna get married.*"

She looked at the camera and he was struck by her direct gaze, wide, expectant, and joyful, "*Nuh-uh! I'd need a boyfriend before that!*"

"*Oh come on, am I chopped liver?*"

"*Yes!*" she answered brightly, "*Need something to put in the tacos!*"

He was tearing up again, but something felt so beautifully neutral about it. Thumbing the tears out of his eyes, he kept scrolling. Shoua showed him a pic that Laura took of him crashed on the couch—with various things carefully balanced on him. Vel quite firmly informed her that Laura did not remove those after the picture, and when he woke up he scared himself when they all toppled off. He had thought it was either a rattlesnake, or a scorpion and her babies! Shoua's smile appeared again, followed up by discreet rubbing of her eyes. Vel shared pictures in turn, ones he took of Laura in both artistic and goofy ways. One picture would be of her looking so warm and thoughtful in the Arizona sunset, another would have a glob of sunscreen on her nose he posted without telling her it was there. Shoua shared a picture of their first dorm room with a fresh-faced Laura grinning at her desk, yet unaware of the strain of college life. Vel gawked when he saw the state of his apartment when he had met Laura—yes truly he had lived like that, and still she dated him with the patience of a saint. Another picture. Another. His chest hurt, but it was a good hurt.

Eventually he found himself stilled on her profile page, just staring at what she chose to display to the world. To his side Shoua had buried her face in her hands, her phone face-down in her lap. Both their smiles had gone. Vel stared. Her profile pic was of the two of them, her wrapped around his chest to smile up at the camera he was also smiling at. Truly, their relationship was no secret. More than once people had erroneously categorized them as fiancés, and...they were, in a sense. Just not officially. But also they weren't, and he thought of the puffed up tortilla with regret. Would it have hurt more if they were finalized, 'official'?

Shoua stood up and hurried back into the house, shielding her eyes from him. Vel kept staring at Laura's profile, his mind waking up and digging.

He searched for Diana Berkeley. There wasn't much to see that wasn't locked, but like Laura her husband was in her profile picture, dark skin to light skin. They were more official than Vel and Laura had been, at least according to court. But something else bothered him. Idly he tapped the edge of his phone.

Then he got up and went back into the house too. The hallway bathroom's light was on and he heard the sink's water rush, but he paid it no mind. Vel beelined to the coffee table and swatted garbage off of the case file.

Alyssa Munroe, her profile also showed her hand in hand with a man of darker complexion. Katie Gutierrez, ditto. Chelsea Benoit, yes her too—not her profile picture but her cover photo. Most of their posts were understandably locked, but he had seen well more than enough. Curiosity turned into coincidence turned into correlation.

And, Katie's final post beyond the mourning on her wall was an excited reveal of an ultrasound photo. Vel looked up to where he had dropped Laura's ultrasound on the floor. *Coincidence.* He reminded himself. *Coincidence.*

Just like how Emily being pregnant was coincidental. It means nothing.

A whole, whole lot of nothing. Three women being pregnant within a year of each other surely, surely...

Vel rubbed his eyes, not noticing Shoua emerge from the bathroom. Without acknowledging her he re-searched the other names and started painstakingly reading the posts he could see. One on Chelsea's page said *I hope you and the little one are safe in heaven.* Vel's heart pounded. Three's company, four's a crowd. Laura did love coincidences, so, so much—

"Um, should you have that uh. Out, Vel?"

Vel blinked, looked at Shoua and stared because she had removed all her makeup and the eyebrow piercing. Shoua awkwardly gestured to the open file on the table. It took him a moment before he yelped and piled every autopsy report back into the manila envelope. Shoua graciously pretended not to notice his snafu and rounded the back of the couch. She also pretended not to notice Vel laying Laura's ultrasound flat as he pulled up Katie's page again, turning on the TV and her PlayStation.

He didn't know if it was just as he thought, but—Laura and Katie shared the same doctor, printed at the very top of their photos. Dr. Randall Thompson. Vel picked up his phone and searched, pulling up an OB/GYN clinic. He squinted—it was near the mall where Laura had requested to be dropped off and picked up from a couple of times. And he had been none the wiser, and *he* was supposed to be the private investigator.

Vel hid a sigh and flipped back to the tab with Chelsea's page. Her partner—husband? Stared back at him, black skin, warm smile.

Curiosity to coincidence to correlation...and perhaps causation.

It was far too late to call tonight, but he took one of the crumpled up napkins on the coffee table, smoothing it in his big hands as he stood up and hunted for a pen.

"Vel?" Shoua said, her eyes glued to the game she was playing but sitting far too stiff to be relaxed, "You're making me nervous."

"Yeah, almost done," he replied absentmindedly.

"*Really* nervous." she drove home. Vel made a short noise of triumph as he finally found a pen and quickly returned to the table.

"Yeah, I—Almost done, I promise." His mind was on fire, he had to get it out. After jotting down the information for the OB/GYN and Chelsea's partner he bit the top of the pen, thinking.

The pen slid into the usual spot, resting in the gap between his upper canine and premolar.

"*Vel,*"

"Yes—Done, done done done." In a quick move to cover everything, he slipped both the napkin note and Laura's ultrasound into the case file and closed it. Out of sight—mostly. He could tell Shoua was eyeing it warily.

"...Are you...what was...Why, did," she struggled to ask.

Vel leaned back, finally looking at the TV, "All the victims were white, including Laura. Turns out all their partners weren't. And from their profiles, some were also pregnant that I can tell, and...Well. It's just coincidence."

He stopped himself very deliberately. Say anything more and it'd rope Shoua further in, and she didn't deserve it—never asked for it, not truly. She made a small *oh* and kept playing. Vel wished he had a way to say *don't worry about it* without sounding condescending.

"What is this?" he asked, changing the subject. Shoua, bless her truly, did not sound affronted by the question.

"Skyrim."

"Oh. Yeah, it is." Vel had seen it before at friend's places and on the internet. Growing up he had only been able to have an original Gameboy well into the mid-2000's. His single working mother couldn't afford much else except what they could find at thrift stores, but at least he was quite entertained by Tetris. She had been dropping hints for a good while that if he helped her save up money that perhaps they could get a new console for him by his thirteenth birthday—handheld, but still far more relevant than he had been to his friends.

But, of course, that didn't pan out. He had the money he had personally saved for a while, but felt ill when thinking of buying anything without her. Especially when he dreamed so often of the colorful new games he'd tell her about, whereas his tía had a very...conservative approach to such things. It just wasn't as fun to tell someone about anything when they'd turn every minuscule detail into a lecture or lesson.

As a result, he sucked at video games. But he was content to watch Shoua. Slowly he melted into relaxation, curling his spine so his long legs ran perpendicular to the couch and away from her. Shoua didn't speak much, although she did mention that she was playing this decade-old game because she didn't have to think through it. The hint was taken, it was a game perfect for muting depression. Better to do this than nothing at all. For that, he was jealous that games were a part of her life.

Before he knew it, his eyelids grew heavy and he fell asleep.

8

Vel drifted awake, groaning. It was still dark, save for the TV being on. He lifted a hand to rub his face and found that the sarape on the back of the couch had been draped over him.

"What time is it?"

Shoua paused and checked, "Almost 5:30."

He blinked rapidly, realizing it wasn't quite as dark as he thought with the early morning washing the rest of the room in a comfortable blue. Then other details; that even with his legs angled off the couch he still took up more than half of it and Shoua had been lounging on one third of the cushions this whole time.

"Shit," he tried to sit up faster than his body was awake, fumbling and trying to rub the sleep away, "You haven't *slept*,"

Shoua shrugged, "It's fine."

"No, the couch—,"

"I get off after midnight most nights. I'm fine."

"But...five in the morning?" he asked dumbly, his voice thick with sleep.

"That's my usual bedtime."

"So," he pushed himself up further, "You should sleep."

She was quiet, then finally said in a much fainter voice, "I'm not tired."

81

Vel stared helplessly as her character moved forward again, traveling on foot with no town or place to rest in sight. He didn't know if that really mattered in Skyrim, but Shoua certainly wasn't wrapping things up any time soon.

"You should at least...have the couch to yourself." he muttered. Shoua shrugged again.

"I can fit. What about you? You slept like...at a right angle."

"I'll put my feet in your lap next time." he threatened.

She scoffed, "No you won't. You go off the edge, don't you?"

He grunted, low and raspy. Yeah, so, what about it. Furthermore, how could she not be tired after such a night, such a week? He could pass out again without warning. Adjusting the sarape around his shoulders, he continued rubbing the sleep from his eyes and yawning. Shoua asked if he was going to bed, and he replied that he should, but...all he did was re-position himself. Wrapped up like a decrepit, long cocoon, Vel wordlessly watched her play until sleep claimed him again. The next time he woke up the TV was off and Shoua was gone. Whether or not she ever slept Vel didn't know, and he was afraid if he asked the answer would depress him.

* * *

There really was nothing grosser than cold sunny side up eggs on toast, but Vel was letting them cool as the phone rang in his ear. He had been playing investigative phone tag as the eggs cooked, which really wasn't that great of an idea if he wanted to enjoy the best breakfast he'd had in a while, but, well, the Tajin should make up for it in the end. Sneaking bites where he could in the midst of phone calls worked up until this point—if this call connected he didn't want to be caught swallowing a mouthful down.

Which is, of course, exactly what happened. A deep, smooth voice answered, vaguely accented in a way that sounded French but not quite European. Vel hid a choke in his shoulder as he forced the food down and cleared his throat.

"Is this uh, Jean Benoit?"

"Yes," he replied courteously.

"Hi, do you have time to talk? My name is Jerónimo Velasquez, I—," he started out quite professional, but stopped suddenly and gave a very loaded sigh that he hoped was disarming as he dropped the façade, "I'm a private investigator. This is about your partner, Chelsea."

The line went quiet for a long time and Vel braced himself for it to cut, but Jean finally relented, "Give me a moment."

"Sure." Vel listened to the muffling of fabric and vague voices in the background. He stole another bite of cold egg on toast. A door opened, then closed, and Jean's voice returned.

"You're investigating her murder, correct?" he asked, not quite closed off but he could hear the hesitation in his voice. Vel had already dropped his pretenses and went full in.

"Yes, I...I'm not gonna lie to you, it's personal on my end too. I'm sorry to bring it up, but grateful that you can talk."

"I don't know what to say that I haven't already said," Jean confessed, then after a moment of thinking added, "But you aren't the cops, so maybe this is better."

Vel laughed dryly, "I'll try. This is gonna hurt but, was...Do you know if Chelsea was pregnant at the time?"

Another long bout of silence. Vel eyed the egg toast. The counter space had been shared time and time again in the morning, making breakfast next to or for each other. Some days one or the other would come home and find them fixing a snack. Sometimes he kissed the top of her head, a quick peck in greeting. Sometimes it was her neck, reciprocated with more and more skin to put his lips on. His height was perfect if she turned and slid onto the counter, legs wide and beckoning. Laura's lips on his, then his neck, jaw, following up to his ear and being tickled if he was wearing a dangling earring that day. The cute, breathy laughter that followed. The shrill, happy sigh after that.

How much harder would it be for her to hop up onto the counter with her belly rounded outward? Laura would certainly keep trying until it was proved impossible, laughing bright even under exertion. All the better for getting up, but what about getting down? He'd have to stoop to brace her legs and back to help with that. Not that he would know.

Suddenly, his appetite dropped.

"Yes...," Jean answered, pulled into the same sorrow that had just washed over Vel, "She was. The police didn't mention that. I didn't think to."

"They didn't mention it to me, either," his mouth felt ashen, the words burning as they left, "Listen, uh, do you remember the name of her OB/GYN? Any details about that at all? There might be a connection."

"No, I don't," Jean paused, "I might have something at home,"

"Did you drive her to the appointments?" Vel asked.

"Yes."

"Was it the one near Park Place?"

"Yes—yes, actually, yes. That's the one."

Vel bit his lip, "You don't have to rush, but when you get home if you have anything confirming which doctor saw her, I'd like to have it. That, and any other administrative details—you might have to call the place and ask. Not her medical records, just the back-end stuff."

Jean agreed, and Vel once more apologized for the intrusion. Rather than hang up, though, he waited, and so did Jean—though it seemed to him that he was lost in thought.

"We moved here to finish my master's. I was hoping to graduate and go home with that *and* a child. More things than my hands could hold," he paused, and Vel felt the air shift, twisting with pain and regret, "Now I'm gonna have nothing."

Gently, Vel asked, "Your degree?"

"That piece of paper?" he responded dismissively, "*Nothing.* Can't build her a house if she ain't there to see it!"

Vel pressed the back of his hand to his eyes, then said, "She hadn't even told me she was pregnant yet, y'know. I found out last night from a friend. On accident."

Both men held a shaky moment of silence.

Pinching his nose hard to pull himself back to the present moment, Vel cleared his throat, "Is it alright if I keep in touch, Jean? About this, I mean."

"Yes. Please." In his emotional fervor Jean's accent had thickened, but it quickly retreated back into it's standardized shell, shielding Vel from truly placing it. If he had to guess, it was from Louisiana...though he was unsure if it was fully Creole or not. His anthropology degree could only do so much when he was born and raised in Tucson, likely never to move away.

"Cool, yeah. You've been a big help, really." Vel rested against the counter and sighed, looking down at his breakfast, "You're busy, right? I won't keep you."

Vel hung up, forcing down his even colder eggs on toast. He

pulled up the OB/GYN's address as he got dressed, trying hard not to let his thoughts wander as he sat on the edge of his side of the bed.

After that, he put a single feather earring in his right ear. When it ghosted his jaw he liked to imagine it as Laura, attempting to kiss him through the rhythm he had set.

If she found out he was chasing coincidences, Lieu would have his head and serve it back to him. He *could* easily say he hired himself to investigate privately, or that hunches led police investigations all the time. (For once he wouldn't say it was to an embittering lack of avail, but he could already see Lieu's cold eyes narrowing in suspicion.) Hell, he could even throw Shoua under the bus. Out of everything he'd done to her recently that'd be the least offensive choice thus far. Regardless, if he could come up with harder evidence to support the coincidences, enough to pique Lieu's intuition, then it'd be worth it—even if he did solve it all alone.

Whether or not that caused the headache he couldn't tell, but he felt out of sorts as he entered the clinic. It was a small, comfortable space; white walls with wide photographs of flowers to add color to the waiting room. Vel couldn't decide if flowers were crass or some sort of O'Keefian nudge and wink. Given the line of pamphlets on the wall that hawked contraceptives and whatever the doctor was pushing out (besides babies), he was leaning towards crass.

Vel swallowed the previous night's panic, tamping it down with inexplicable bad tastes in the mouth. Waiting in line was itself its own torture, because the longer he kept in his own head the more scrambled the anxiety became, desperate to escape. Business. He was here on business. In his pocket there was the note with Laura and Shoua's handwriting as his piece of evidence. Vel thumbed its edge, damning himself for ruining the corners but taking comfort in it all the same.

The receptionist looked fresh out of college but not new to the job. She greeted him cordially and without prejudice, though there was guarded air between her and Vel. He cleared his throat and tried to appear as friendly as possible when he loomed well over the average height.

"Alright, I...Listen uh, my girlfriend passed away very recently and I'd like to recover her records." he stood dumbly, letting the receptionist's manufactured frown of sympathy hit him like a brick.

As gently as she could without losing her guard, she responded, "So she was your girlfriend, not engaged or married?"

Vel swallowed, "Right."

She typed on the computer for a while even though he had not yet given her any details. He stood quietly. *Goodly,* he hoped. Thank god he had the wherewithal to not wear Catholic affects—he leaned more towards the memory of his mother today, and thus wore her old necklace. Although adorning his neck and breast with a rat's skull bordered by quail feathers wasn't exactly friendly, it held less of a contemptuous reaction in this kind of clinic.

"May I have her name?"

"Laura Piper." It was a weight on his tongue. More typing.

"And your name?"

"Jerónimo Velasquez." Silence as the receptionist quietly looked through documents.

"...Sorry, I can't give that information out."

Vel curled his fingers on the counter. *What? How?* He was Laura's emergency contact for her other medical records, as well as her for his. But this—she must've figured he would've gotten nosy at some point (as he always did) and protected whatever she could in order to surprise him. In order to surprise him! It was the most benign, saccharine reasoning but all the sweetness in the world would not help him with legality here.

Goddammit, Laura. He rubbed his feverish brow and grimaced, "Uh, who *is* the emergency contact? Shoua Xiong? Spelled S-H-O—,"

"I'm sorry, I can't give that information out." The receptionist's voice remained professional, but at his persistence she had grown colder and harder. On a better, clearer day Vel would've taken a hint.

As it were, his panic was unraveling and sharpening his voice, "Look, *please*, she was murdered about a month ago and I had no idea she was pregnant until Shoua—her best friend—told me last night. I just want records, her ultrasound, a picture, *anything*. I can prove she was going to tell me, here—,"

"Sir," she was calm and collected, but did not take her eyes off of him, "In the event of a death if you're a family member or the owner of her estate we can release the files to you. But as it stands, I'm sorry, contact someone in her family."

Suddenly, with all the pressure of a waterfall, Vel felt the horrific weight of what Shoua had chosen. To tell Laura's parents, those genuinely benevolent people, that their little girl had not only been murdered but was secretly *pregnant* at the time? It would be a nightmare to see their faces. A nightmare he saw unfold on Shoua the night before.

There was one loophole he could think of and he swore at himself. He did not *want* to bring it up, but if he had to he had to, "Unless it's police business, correct?"

The receptionist quirked an eyebrow, "Is it?"

Vel was well aware he now looked like a desperate ass, "Well, private investigation. Vested interest, too, obviously."

"There are a lot of people with *vested* interests in what happens around here," the receptionist coolly responded, "Now sir, please, if you don't have the relevant information then I cannot help you."

"Here," Vel pulled out his wallet, "My ID. You can pull up my P.I. registration. I can wait while you run it and see where we're at afterward. Alright?"

She stared at him and leveled a response, "I'll see if Dr. Strong is around to talk to you."

"Yeah, thanks." Vel said, stepping away from the counter. She stood up and dipped into the back while the receptionist next to her gave him a peripheral glance. Oh, they could pretend, but he had looked at the roster of doctors that worked here; there was no such person as Dr. Strong. It had to be code for the scene he was causing. He puffed a breath of frustration and looked around the waiting room for a seat.

Someone waved at him and he started in shock, for the briefest of terrifying moments seeing her as Laura. When he regained reality he squinted in confusion, then recognition. The pregnant woman he had pulled from the sinkhole—Emily, that was her name. A hot wash of sheepishness swept over him and he awkwardly slunk over.

"Hey, I thought I recognized you," she greeted, a little tired but otherwise sweet. There was a marked difference about her now that she wasn't whimpering in terror and soaked to the bone. In the light it was even more obvious just how far along she was and the toll the stress was taking on her. *What a coincidence to meet her here,* "Having problems?"

"Uh," he glanced over his shoulder at the receptionist's desk, "Yup. Ugly ones, too." He turned back to her and gave a small gesture at her belly, "Everything alright with you, Emily? After last night I mean."

Her face lit up at the remembrance of her name and she adjusted in her seat to something he hoped was more comfortable, but she didn't seem confident, "That's what I'm here to find out, actually. I don't think so but...can never be too careful."

Vel slumped into the chair next to her, "Yeah. I feel that."

"What about you? ...Vel, was it?"

"That's me. One and only," he sighed, "It's uh, not a pretty story."

"I'm sorry. Is your girlfriend having problems?"

"I mean, she's dead. Biggest problem yet." he looked over and saw Emily's pale, horrified reaction.

"I'm so sorry—she...I don't remember her name, but—,"

"Her name? Why would you—," When it hit him he scrunched his eyes tight and rubbed them with a hand. It'd be something to torment Shoua with later, but for now he was the one receiving psychic damage, "Oh, *no.* No, Shoua and I are just friends. Laura was my girlfriend. She was killed about a month and a half ago."

Emily gave a quiet *oh,* sitting with one hand on her belly and staring dimly across the floor.

"Found out last night when we got home safe that uh, she had been pregnant and she hadn't told me yet. So I'm here to get files, but there's...complications." Another glance to the reception, still single-staffed. Even though his hand was pitched against his brow it felt like the remaining receptionist was on so high of an alert she knew he was staring.

"God...," Emily curled her fingers on her belly, "I can't

imagine."

He heaved a sigh, trying not to wince that it was audibly staggered and fragile, "Can't blame 'em, can I? Bet they deal with angry jealous boyfriends all the time. And I'm not exactly a cakewalk right now. Or so everyone's been telling me."

"For what it's worth, you were very nice."

He looked over at her, "Oh yeah?"

"I told my boyfriend I was glad you were. I don't think I would've kept my head about me if not."

A smile crooked up Vel's cheeks. There was a damning sincerity in Emily's voice, made moreso by a deeply controlled breath. Vel had a moment of gratitude in return; whatever dominoes had fallen so that she had *not* gone into early labor with her lower half sunken in road water needed to be framed and praised. For as much as he could count himself to spring to action, that action was nothing if not instinct and his instinct around pregnant women could be justly defined as *stupid*, if only because he hadn't had to ever deal with them.

Emily's phone screen lit up before his smile could fall, displaying a picture of her next to her partner. He had ruddy hair and pale skin, smiling enough to show off crow's feet at the corners of his eyes.

"That him?" Vel asked, keeping the subject alive, "Is he a good guy?"

"Yes, we're very excited—," Emily paused, "And very worried."

"Good," Vel accepted, pulling Laura's pendant from his pocket and absently twirling it until the cord wrapped tight around his finger to unwind and repeat, "Your doctor here good too?"

"*Yes*, thank goodness. It's been a long, *long* process and Dr.

Dillon has been kind the whole way." No wonder they as a couple were worried, no wonder Emily had found a way to push through whatever fear she surely felt last night.

Vel then let out a breath involuntarily, feeling *some* relief that certainly, certainly Laura had done her research and heard good things about this clinic. Ignoring the somewhat prying look Emily gave him, he continued on casually.

"What about Dr. Thompson?"

"Him? I think he's fairly new. I don't know much about him at all."

Vel tightened his jaw and released it, "Oh."

"Listen...," Emily said after a short, awkward silence, "If you need me to vouch for your character, I think I can do that a little, y'know? As a thank you."

Vel laughed dryly since she knew just about as much as the receptionists did, "Well, thanks. I think just you being here helps more than you know."

"I mean, what a coincidence!" she remarked.

"Yeah," Vel echoed distantly, "What a coincidence."

A nurse called Emily back and she rose to her feet. Before waddling off, she bid Vel a quick *good luck*. Vel spread his fingers out and sent a wave through them in acknowledgment.

"Right back at ya."

He felt her absence immediately, suddenly back into the light of scrutiny that would justifiably be harsh on him. The pendant spun, he snatched it out of its arc, released it, spun it again. He had lied about not having an ultrasound in an attempt to gain headway into the files at all, but that may have been a mistake—if he had said he had it, he could've persuaded that Laura would've wanted him to have her records. A thought annoyed him. In the heat of the conversation he had simply accepted that Laura simply didn't want him to know so to better surprise him, but Laura wouldn't lack caution. Release forms were for these exact sort of situations, and the thought that she hadn't laid down his name...

No. *No*, it was impossible. Laura had eagerly told Shoua and spent the whole time planning out how to reveal the baby to him at all. There was no way, *no goddamn way* she had cheated. It hurt him to even *think* of it, but the more he yelled at himself for such horrible thoughts the harder those thoughts took hold of him.

Unless, of course, there was something worse. Vel was going to make himself throw up. Surely Laura would've told him if she had been raped. He didn't mean it to be callous either, because in the days leading up to her death everything was as normal as ever. If anything Laura was chipper and bright in a way that was more infectious than usual. Perhaps he was subconsciously picking up on her pregnant glow. Nausea ravaged him. *Why, Laura? Why?*

"Mr. Velasquez?"

Vel looked up. Standing above him was a tall, slim man with graying blond hair and hazel eyes. His tie was a splash of color against his white coat and he held a clipboard quite casually against his chest. His smile was wide and effortlessly cordial, but there was something pointed about his gaze that told Vel he was watching his every move.

"Dr. Thompson. I understand you have questions concerning releasing patient records?"

"That's correct." Vel carefully said, snatching up Laura's pendant and holding it firm in his palm, "Sorry for the trouble."

"Well if we can get this sorted out then there won't be trouble, will there?" his grin remained, almost customer service in how it glowed, "Why don't we discuss it in my office?"

Vel stole a glance around the waiting room. The other receptionist had returned, and though there was a break in patients—likely to coincide with lunch hours—there was a car pulling up into the lot. Dealing with a difficult person behind closed doors so as to not stress the already stressed out patients made sense. But the pendant in his palm trembled, and not in a way that seemed excited at the prospect.

Still, Vel got up, reveling a little in the raising of Dr. Thompson's eyebrows as he stood noticeably above his height.

"Sure," Vel said, forcing his voice to be neutral, "Lead the way."

Contrary to what he expected—although he didn't know what to expect—Dr. Thompson led him into an examination room. He bid Vel to take a seat and he did, bewildered and staring at the table just off to the side. Overall, he supposed it saved space to have both things be one and the same though there was nothing but medical supplies and no hints of records. Even so it was hard to take his eyes off of the stirrups, imagining, knowing that Laura had been in this very room. Her ankles were likely set right where he was staring, chatting cordially during the exam. He wondered how she sounded—she chatted when she was both comfortable and uncomfortable, the only indication from one over the other was the speed and tone of her voice. He vaguely remembered discussions surrounding how cold the instruments were—did they warm them up here? Was she...did she do alright?

"Now then," Dr. Thompson interrupted his thoughts, and he thankfully pulled his eyes away, "You're only looking for the reports from a Laura Piper, correct?"

"Yes," Vel answered, level, "She's deceased. I just want...I want to see the ultrasound. How she did here, if possible."

"Sorry to hear that," Dr. Thompson said without looking up from the clipboard. It hit Vel like a light punch to the chest—he was used to words of sympathy by this point, but none had been delivered quite so...distantly. It was imperative to keep his cool, it was imperative to remember what he looked like in this stark white room: A jealous, potentially dangerous boyfriend. After all, he hadn't quite said *how* Laura died. Suspicion could easily sink him here, "But there is no Jerónimo Velasquez to release to."

"I know," Vel said, rasping and weak, "I don't want to cause a scene."

"Well, I can offer some suggestions," Dr. Thompson smiled, "Save you a trip to a lawyer's office. If you get in contact with her closest living relatives, perhaps her parents or a sibling, we could release the files to them. Otherwise, there's not much to do for decades yet."

Same as the receptionist said, but now Vel had been sequestered off into a place that sucked much of his power in arguing, "I appreciate it."

"Technically, you know more than we're supposed to let on by assuming she was a patient here at all," he continued.

"That's my job," Vel said, trying to crack some humor into the room but the only one smiling was the doctor, "I snoop."

"So your license deems," Dr. Thompson's voice dipped ever so slightly. Vel would've missed it were it not for the shift of the pendant in his palm, as if it was lifting an ear to the conversation, "But surely we don't need to get the authorities involved here. I don't think they'd look favorably in your direction."

Shit. If Dr. Thompson had gotten the bright idea to notify Lieu, he was in worse hell than temporary suspension. Lieu had stood up for him more times than she should've, but that well was sure to run dry when he was making mistake after mistake in front of her, giving baldfaced proof that he wasn't fit for work.

If that wound up climbing the ladder above her, there wasn't much she would or could do to keep him on official cases. It wouldn't be the end of the world, but it would mean that he'd flounder. Without Laura's income he didn't have the luxury of rest and would likely return to his part-time job making beds at a golf resort. Not the end of the world, not the end of the *world*, but the dissolution of another relationship was *not* something he wanted to happen. Especially when his friendship with Shoua was so painfully precarious—thanks to him, thanks to mistake after mistake.

"Oh, don't worry," Dr. Thompson soothed in a voice that seemed to revel the way Vel had when he stood taller than him, "We haven't contacted the authorities just yet—it's something we'd like to avoid as much as you would, I assume."

Ugh. He was only good at putting up a poker face if he wasn't so—*this*, this emotional and messy. If he could joke and feign his incompetence, he'd be fine. Instead it felt like the good doctor here had sniffed out his vulnerability, and unfortunately he saw deeper than Vel wanted to admit. His eyes flicked to the examination table, having a hard time being focused on anything else.

"Listen," Vel tried, "If there is someone on the release form, can you send the records to them?"

Dr. Thompson tapped a pen against the clipboard, his gaze boring hard and his smile more distant than before, "Usually we do that at *that* person's request, not someone else's."

"She's dead," Vel argued, "Shouldn't the forms be sent out anyway? You know, *released?*"

Tap, tap, tap. Dr. Thompson was regarding him *very* critically all of the sudden, and Vel pulled away from the examination table to stare directly back. The rule of dogs, the first to look away now was the loser.

"If you're that unfamiliar with HIPAA, Mr. Velasquez, you should leave our practices to us."

Frustration welled in him and he retorted, "I have a right to know. The person on the release form has a right to know."

"You aren't her spouse, nor on the release form. These rules are in place to protect the women we see—and while I don't mean to *imply* anything, they're to protect them from...*snooping* eyes."

Vel stared.

"Yeah I don't think you saved me a trip to a lawyer after all."

Dr. Thompson rolled his lips inward on his smile, "I suppose that's your choice to make. Now please, leave quietly or I'll have to force you to leave—and that would result in an incident report. Which could escalate." The look was pointed, *again*, *something you wouldn't want*. He stood up and Vel stood too, the momentary break of eye contact unwelcome. The pendant in his palm hurt to hold though he wasn't squeezing it any harder than before.

"I'll let you know two things: One, that I assure you Miss Piper did not die due to medical malpractice—anyone who saw the news report would agree, no one could've done that to her."

Vel's lip curled for a half-second. He was unsure if it was from the doctor's words or the biting sting of the pendant breaking his flesh.

"Two, and this is just between us: She was a very sweet young woman. It's a shame, and I feel what you're feeling. Now please, leave my office and the clinic."

He opened the door and waited. Vel stilled for a moment. When he moved he tensed, as if he was expecting to be pounced upon despite the promise that security hadn't been called. Even when he was out into the hall he didn't duck his head down like he normally would, far too alert.

Vel's mind buzzed like he had missed something but couldn't remember what. When he got to the lobby he opened the palm of his hand to see a smattering of red staining the pendant. The edges were still smoothed down, unable to cut anything—much less skin. There were no chips in the stone, nothing that could've actually cut him (nothing that could've actually hurt her, he wouldn't allow it, he made it that way for a reason). His mind was too clouded to think properly, hardly understanding the blood beyond the feeling the doctor gave him. Odd. Like that should've gone differently, but he couldn't tell how without feeling petty. His tía would scold him for being selfish in the wake of a professional. His gut...his gut thought of his mother's eyes looking up at him from their open case, coaxing him to draw the answers himself.

Wary of the set of eyes on him, he sped up and out of the clinic. The breath he released was not as full of relief as he wanted it to be. Despite the temperature, he shivered under the partly cloudy sky and rubbed his face with his clean hand. He had to relax, unscramble his mind somehow. That meant a cigarette. Vel dug one out, moving towards his car as he did so because of all the things he needed today being further scrutinized by the clinic for smoking in front of pregnant women was *not* one of them.

He passed a truck, thought nothing of it, then paused. There was still dust all over the chassis, which was not exactly an anomaly if the driver happened to have an overhang if not a garage. What *was* an anomaly was a break in the dust. On the hood there were several places where fingers had laid, popping it up over and over again. Vel stared. The truck was younger than his car, though it could've been a lemon. However, there was more than one set of fingers. It was hard to tell since finger oils smeared the dust, but he was almost certain that some sets were smaller than others. Shorter, for sure.

He blinked. Perhaps it was just the lemon's oil that he was smelling, but the metallic wafting scent near the truck seemed different than a car engine's.

"Oh, Vel!"

Thankful that he had not bled that much, he closed his hand around the pendant, jammed the cigarette in his mouth, and turned to see Emily.

"Hey, how did it go?" he asked before she could.

"Nothing obvious just yet," she answered, and her lack of suspicion made some tension leave his shoulders.

"I guess that's a good sign," Vel said hopefully, "You made it this far and that's the hard part, right?" He pulled his lighter out, stopping the habitual motion before lighting it.

"God, I suppose so," Emily adjusted her purse on her shoulder, "What about you? Do you need me to vouch for you?"

"Uh," he glanced back at the clinic, but the reflection of the clouds in the windows deterred him from seeing inside, "No I think...It's fine."

"You sure?" she asked, even though he had he scooted over to his car and opened the door.

"Yeah I...it's messy, right? I'll be better about it once I clear my head." he said, squeezing the pendant as he leaned against his door. Changing the subject quickly so she wouldn't have time to think yet again, he asked, "What are you gonna name your kid?"

"Oh—we've got a few ideas," *yes, mission accomplished for once,* "As a matter of fact, what *is* your name?"

"What, Vel isn't cool enough?" he smirked. Emily furrowed her brows in amusement.

"It's short for something, isn't it?"

"Short for Jerónimo."

"What? *How?*"

The smirk turned into a grin wide enough to show the gaps on either side of his teeth. He patted the top of his car door, "Jerome works. Seeya around Emily—," he paused halfway into his car and bid, "Stay safe."

She must've said good-bye to him in turn, but he willfully missed it as he turned on his car and sped out of the parking lot with a numb stare.

Shoua was still not in the house when he returned, and though it dealt a hollow punch to his chest he couldn't let himself blame her. The last thing she needed (and really the last thing he needed) was to be cornered together again. The last two times it had happened he had put his tongue down her throat and unwittingly forced a secret she had never meant to tell. He had gotten dangerously close to doing something irreversible, and Shoua? Well he couldn't quite know what she was thinking, but her aversion to him was clear.

Unlike how it had been before, being home scrambled his brain *more*, confusing fact with emotion. The resting pace of his heartbeat felt faster than normal, and taking any note of that made it race faster. He groaned and checked the fridge.

Not great.

Super not great.

He couldn't even put together a decent sandwich with what he had—though he had to face it, he couldn't do that even if he had all the ingredients anyway. Vel sighed and went through the usual routine—lunch meat and cheese straight from the package, some honey drizzled on toast from cheap bread. Tea— tea would be good. Relaxing tea. Tea that would lull him to sleep. He made chamomile, standing at the counter while the water heated.

Well. He didn't make chamomile, he simply put the bag in the water. His mother had her way with chamomile to the point that manzanilla was one of the Spanish words he retained. He scrunched his face. The times where she made it the best were when he was at his most feverish and couldn't remember what she had done to the tea. Fresh chamomile flowers he knew, but it was more than that...A hint of lemon, perhaps, and maybe something minty, but none of the mint he ever found in the store fulfilled the particular flavor she had managed to work into the tea.

Hell. All of it. And so much more effort than he could do at the moment anyway.

Store bought chamomile was fine. It did the job. Vel meandered around the house, poking his head into the spare bedroom. Here he had the desk ready for the ofrenda. For the time being much of his mother's things resided there as well, nestled next to strongboxes with case information and files. The case that held her eyes was where it always was at the foot of a picture of her. Part of him wished he had a picture of his father because there were times where he felt like he didn't look like his mother. Yes, her face was wide and her nose big, her lips always had a ghost of a smile, and her hair was loosely crinkled like his. But she wasn't particularly tall nor scrawny like him, her skin was far lighter, and her eyes were a deep and calming brown, not strikingly blue-green. Over the years he had come to joke that they were his award-winning *National Geographic* eyes, but deep down (perhaps not that deep) he was frustrated that he looked like a stranger.

Though she had always said with awe, moreso and moreso the older he got, that he looked so much like him. She'd clasp his cheeks and remark on his unique beauty. *Is it a blessing or a curse that you have your father's eyes?* And Vel, not understanding the gravity of her grief, would chirp that it was a blessing, *of course it was a blessing, Mom.* Her resolve would crack into a warm smile, brought to the present by his innocence. In those moments he had to figure that she had loved him regardless.

His tía complained about that. More than once he caught a bitter *odio al indio ese* under her breath after making eye contact with him. More than once she lamented that he didn't inherit his mother's beautiful brown eyes like he *should* have. Vel had nothing to say to counter it. He was too busy being a distraught kid, later a rebellious and angry teen. There were other problems to worry about and far greater problems to give her. But every time he heard *odio al indio* he defiantly remembered the warmth of his mother's hands and her melting smile.

Still, he wished he looked more like her.

Laura respectfully never asked about his father, nor the case he was so careful to keep next to the photograph of his mother. Likely she thought it was a lock of her hair, or perhaps a pair of glasses though she hadn't worn any. Vel thumbed the basic case, nothing fancy, nothing that denoted its worth to him. He took a sip of the tea, willing his closeness to his mother to bring the ingredients he didn't know back into the drink. Even if it was a psychosomatic reaction, he needed it. He needed a lot of things, Mom.

The evening passed well into night. Shoua still didn't return, and by that point he figured she was at work—and would likely go back to her apartment to sleep, having spent the day clearing out as much of the flood as possible before the next torrent of rain. His mug of tea was empty. Vel held onto its emptiness for the rapidly dissipating warmth until he sighed and retreated into the bedroom.

***

it could've been a child's bedroom. it would've been his child's bedroom.

***

Vel awoke with a start. Something, *something* was off, something about the house was holding its breath with him inside it. He pulled his head up from the pillow, listening intently. No rain poured on the roof, no flashes of light followed by distant thunder. But *something* was there. He looked over his shoulder at the rest of the room. Nothing stirred.

But somewhere, something scraped against tile. Low and heavy, like strange shuffling footsteps. Vel, eyes wide, carefully slid his legs out from under the sheets and onto the floor. His feet flexed. It would be quietest to keep them bare. Carefully he crept to the dirty laundry hamper, pulling his old sleep shirt out and over his head. As he did so the noise happened again; steps, something was *roaming* in his house. And it was a some*thing*, not some*one*—no person's footsteps sounded like *that*.

His heart tried to seize his throat. There were bears in the National Parks surrounding Tucson, but to his knowledge they were all relatively small, such as black bears. Even then, there was a *weight* to the steps that he had a hard time attributing to something as big as a grizzly—as if he had ever encountered one to know.

Walking on the balls of his feet, he crept quickly to the door. Thanking himself for having had the lack of care or energy to close it, he gingerly pushed it open and peered down the hallway. He couldn't see, but the roaming noise became sharper.

Then, something in the deep blue of the night shifted into his vision and he bit down on his cheeks to avoid audibly sucking in a breath. It was big—its shoulder must've been as tall as he was—and it was dark, moving like some sort of animal but nothing moved like this that he knew of. Vel pulled back into the bedroom and darted his eyes around. *An unknown beast.*

He had to get out.

Vel snatched Laura's pendant off the end table and unplugged his phone, slipping both into the pocket of his shorts. *How the hell had it gotten in?* A beast of that size would've had to have shattered a window, no, the patio door—why didn't he wake up to a definitive noise? Car keys, car keys—still in his pants pocket from the previous day. Good god he had never been so happy to be depressed. A glance at the time—just past three in the morning.

The shambling stopped and he heard the heavy, deep breathing of something sniffing out its prey. Vel stilled, heart pounding in his ears. Of all the times he had hunched over to make his body smaller to accommodate, this was the one time he truly *needed* to. Slow—slow, he concentrated on the word *slow*, and then *cold*. He bit the inside of his lip so hard it broke, spilling blood in his mouth. *Slow, cold*, and he swallowed his own blood as a desperate exchange.

The sniffing stopped.

Vel stopped. *Slow, cold.* Nothing down here. Nothing down the hallway. Nothing in the bedroom. Stopped still, eyes wide, waiting, listening.

One heavy step, then another. It was turning away from the hallway and back into the living room. Vel sucked in a breath of courage and held his pocket to his thigh to keep from jingling. Keeping close to the walls, he sidled down, inch by inch.

The thing was huge. That was all he could parse, and for the time being it was turned away from him. Vel reached until his fingers wrapped around the edge of the door to the spare room, and, from a stone-still pause, he darted inside.

Once his mother's eyes were in his other pocket, he slowly shut the door as silently as possible. His mind took inventory for him, and he started gathering what he could justifiably hold for what it was worth. Knife. A wreathed effigy woven by his mother from dried willow, spent feathers, and spines. Anything—no, he couldn't hold anything else. Not without spending the dwindling time he had before the beast found him out.

Especially since the next part wasn't so easy. Carefully he wedged a chair under the door handle. Vel then sucked in a breath and placed his hands on the window latches. Counting down, he psyched himself out, counted down again, then flipped them open. The *clack*, though a soft sound, ripped as loud as a gunshot and he raced on frantic instinct with the beast's steps thudding towards him. Vel dragged his knife through the screen and scrambled through, effigy under arm. The door pounded angrily, and Vel toppled onto the ground. Everything snapped into speed. The pain radiating from his shoulder disappeared in a flood of adrenaline. He sprang to his feet and dashed around his backyard to the garage. Behind him the door pounded once, twice, *crashed*, crumbled, and there was a roar of rage.

Nope nope nope nope nope, *not* looking back, Vel jammed himself into his car, revved the engine, and backed out without looking. Speeding down the residential street at a crisp illegal clip, he allowed himself *one* glance in the rearview.

Whatever it was, and he still couldn't tell even with the street lamps, it was *furious*.

Vel floored it and tore through the early morning streets of Tucson, praying he didn't run into a cop, praying he *did* run into a cop, dipping through back streets where he could to avoid street lights. If he drove it into one of the Parks that would get it away from people, but also put his ass on the Missing 411 list no question should it catch up with him, and Vel had no doubt that it *would*.

Just imagine it: His lopsided chapped-lip smile plastered across the boards of conspiracy theorists and true crime en-thusiasts! He *could* think of a worse fate but that alone was enough to keep the accelerator floored.

That being said, he couldn't run forever. He chewed his lip, knowing, just *knowing* what she would say before hard turning in the direction of Shoua's apartment. Now, what she would scream about the beast would be a surprise, but to be honest it was going to be a welcome one.

Bewildered anger darkened her face as Shoua opened the door, his fist flying through the air mid-pound. Vel gave a breathless, inexplicable *hey* and shouldered his way inside.

"Vel, what the *fuck?!* Do you know what time it is?!"

"You were awake, right?" he shoved the door closed with his shoulder, winced in a way that Shoua caught onto, and pulled the knife from its sheath. Her eyes grew wide and she stumbled back as Vel stabbed it into the heart of her door.

"*Vel!!*" Shoua shouted, keeping her distance likely on the assumption that he had lost his mind, "What the actual *fuck* are you *doing?*"

Vel hung the wreath on the knife, panting hard. Delicate bends of willow strung the vertebrae together, the flange of the long thoracic spines running along the length of his arm as he pulled away. What animal had it been? Vel hoped a strong one, because he had two seconds—

"Vel if you don't fucking tell me what's going on I'll call the police, I'll ask for your boss, I'll, I'll,"

—to explain himself—

"Get back," he reached for her and she wrenched away, "Get *back*, away from the door!"

—and one second to—*THUD.*

Shoua skittered back in shock, the other side of the door suddenly *much* worse than him. Vel grabbed her arm and lunged to the far wall, bare feet scraping against the sediment left behind by the floodwaters.

THUD. The bottom of the wreath lurched, but settled back in place. Shoua's nails dug into him, her voice cracking, "You brought it *here?!*"

"I didn't know where else to go!" he protested pathetically. Her nails dug further in with each subsequent thud, watching in terror as the wreath shook with the walls, "It showed up in my *house*, Shoua!"

"It *what?!*" she shrieked, silenced by a thud accompanied by an infuriated roar, "What the *fuck...!*"

Thud after thud weakened their knees, kept upright only by the wall that shook against their backs. Shoua shook her head and bleated, "That...thing, is that, is *that*,"

"Hell if I know," Vel rasped, "...Probably."

"Does that mean it's—," thud, roar, "Following you?!"

Vel laughed, shaky and forced as the thuds sped up one after the other, the beast beating the door like an ape. The laugh caught in his throat, panic spreading as the wreath trembled along the knife's blade. He slipped an arm out from behind Shoua and planted it in front of her, pressing her between him and the wall as if his spindly body was enough to protect anything. But if it really was following *him*, and not her—maybe it would drag him by his legs and leave her alone. Still she readjusted her grip, her nails now digging into his ribs. Vel gripped her hand, ready to pry her off if need be.

Then, silence. Their breaths rasped in haggard confusion, struggling to be quiet enough to listen. The wreath hung from the knife undisturbed. Vel perked his head, eyes darting from window to window—*the windows*—

A dark shape moved in the way of the outdoor light and Vel shouted, grabbing Shoua again. The glass shattered as a long, shaggy arm filled the small basement window and swiped hungrily. Vel scrambled, dragging her to the windowless bathroom. Shoua yelped, half-afraid, half-indignant. The claws of the creature sank into the wall and dragged, ripping lines into the plaster.

Vel slammed the door shut with such force he toppled backwards over Shoua, landing disgracefully on the bathroom floor. She yelped again, tangled and pulled down with him. It was pitch black, but neither got up to turn the light on.

Shoua panted, pushed his leg and arm off of her, then asked, "Are you alright?"

"*Ungh*," he groaned for an answer, much slower to pull himself up. Outside the bathroom the beast raged, back and forth from window to door to other window. As ridiculous as it sounded, that brought Vel the smallest iota of relief; if it was frantically moving from option to option it meant none of them were viable. He squeezed his eyes shut to see colors and sparks dance in his vision. That wreath had the strength of a boar. That was it. Thank fuck.

When it was clear he was *mostly* alright, Shoua continued, "What's going on?"

"You're asking *me?*" Vel pawed around to map the room, brushing against her accidentally and earning a hard slap on his arm.

"*Who* the hell else would I ask?" she snapped. Vel found the wall and used it as support to sit up, feeling the adrenaline slink away into the dark. He gulped down air and answered with sticky lips.

"I don't know. I woke up with it sniffing around and got out as it started chasing me. Then I came here. That's it, I *swear.*"

"*Inside* your house?"

"*Inside* my house." Vel groaned again, nursing his shoulder as the pain from the fall started coming back, "Your stuff is fine, by the way. I think."

"How comforting," she muttered sarcastically.

The beast continued to pace outside, occasionally trying to push its way in. From the sound of her breaths he could tell when Shoua jumped at a noise, which gradually relaxed as time went on and they remained safe in the bathroom.

"That...thing," Shoua said after a while, "If it's really the one that killed Laura...,"

He swallowed on a pained groan, massaging the top of his neck before realizing the tension had already spread to his temples. When he didn't say any words in turn, Shoua decided to keep talking.

"Did you get a good look at it?"

"No," Vel rasped, "I have no idea what it is."

"I thought you were a witch, or something." Shoua wasn't pleased with his answers, but more likely she wasn't pleased he was there at all.

"My *mom*," he corrected with an involuntary scowl, "My *mom* was a bruja. I picked up on some of her habits, I have *no idea* what works or doesn't or what goes on or what's what or *anything*."

Despite the dark he could see Shoua pale before accusing, "So, you had—when you put the wreath on the door, you,"

"No fucking clue what I was doing, yeah, got it in one," he groaned again, finally acknowledging that his head was throbbing and he was dying for a cigarette in the wake of all the adrenaline, "I didn't want the thing to break through the door, I put up something that looked protective, I thought real hard about it, and it worked. Right? We're still alive."

"*Christ...*," Shoua swore under her breath in awe over his audacity.

"No, that was my tía. Actually, saying a few Hail Marys doesn't sound so bad right now."

"Are you serious?! Do you understand how hard I'm freaking out?!"

"*Yes*," Vel snapped back, "And what about how *I* feel? Waking up with *that* in my fucking house?!"

"*You're* the one who brought it here! Why are you getting mad at *me* for being upset?!"

"*Shoua*," he grit his teeth on every word, "I. Need. A. Cigarette. So bad."

Shoua quieted, and he could feel her eyes on him—hard and upset but behind that sympathetic. There was a massive advantage to having a bartender as a friend, and it was the lack of judgment and further yet a baseline understanding. He heard the sound of her hands on the cabinets. Vel pulled his phone out and slid it to her with the flashlight on. She grabbed two bottles with its help.

"What's better, ibuprofen or acetaminophen?"

"*Neither*," he spat, sucked his vitriol back in, whined, tried again, "I don't know. Ibuprofen."

Shoua set the acetaminophen down, "When was the last time you ate?"

"Huh? I don't know, what does it matter?" Vel was getting impatient, petulantly so, and it was coming out in his voice.

"You shouldn't have it on an empty stomach," Shoua supplied matter-of-factly, and at the sound of her pulling her feet under her Vel freaked.

"You're *not* going out there!"

"The kitchen is right next to the bathroom, nowhere near any windows." she grunted, annoyed.

"*No.*"

Shoua blew up, "Vel, for fuck's sake, I'm trying to *help*. That's all I've been *doing* this past month and a half! You realize that, don't you? God if you didn't make it so difficult half the time—"

"Shoua, sit—,"

"*No!*" she yelled, the full force of her anger forcing him to shut up, "You don't get to *sit there* and tell me what to do after *everything!!* After sitting and not saying anything for the funeral, after weeks of worrying if you were alive or going to make it through the next day, after putting up with your mess when I didn't even have my *own* shit put together—*no!! Fuck* you, Vel! *Fuck!!!*"

Vel swallowed hard and felt it all the way down into his empty stomach. Shoua flung the bottle of ibuprofen at the ground and he flinched when it bounced up, failing to catch it before it clattered into the shower next to him.

"You drag the *fucking thing* that killed Laura, that *killed Laura!* To my apartment! And think I'm gonna help?? Think I'm gonna be just *okay* with all of this?! *I don't want this Vel!! Any of it!!!*"

"No," Vel struggled to get a word in as a bubble formed in the back of his throat, "I *don't* think that,"

"*I want Laura back!!!*" she screamed.

Vel tilted his chin to the ceiling, stupefied and dizzy. He felt as though he was sinking through the bathroom linoleum, as though he was going to throw up, as though the world was closing overhead. Shoua's voice echoed in the tiny space well after she had stopped shouting. She reduced to choked breaths, anger and hurt painting the dark more than the beast's sounds.

"God, just, fine—whatever, I don't *care* anymore," she was on the verge of sobbing, and upon that realization Shoua turned and put her hand on the doorknob. The sound shot Vel back into the room and he lunged, wrapping his arms around her and flexing them tight. Shoua screamed and struggled, hitting him for release. Vel backed up, pulling her to the floor with him but keeping her trapped. The second she hit the tile her rage tilted and her voice pitched with *fear*. Real, deep, carnal fear. Vel relented just enough until only his hands pinned her arms, but still he didn't let her go.

"You're *not* going out there," he snarled.

"Vel—," Shoua struggled, kicking the air next to him and weakly clawing his arms from the poor angle he had given her, "Let go of me!"

"That thing killed Laura, do you really think I'd let it get to you too?" the rage in his chest burned hot and spread over his skin like a comfortable blanket, assured of its existence. Shoua was not so convinced, her breaths cold and fast, yet still Vel held her, "What would Laura say if I let that happen? *Shoua*,"

"Vel *please*," Shoua begged in a hoarse whisper.

He lifted his hands and slowly retreated, though his gaze was fixed on what he could see of her in the harsh white light from his phone, "No," he said firmly, "It doesn't matter what Laura would say. I won't let it happen. Not if I can help it. Not to *you*."

He pulled his long legs up and wrapped his arms around his knees, finally releasing Shoua in totality by looking away, "Not anyone else."

No one deserved this.

"I want Laura back, too." he said, squeezing his legs until he took up as little space as possible.

In the silence that followed Vel realized that the beast's onslaught had stopped completely. That followed silence was filled with Shoua's staggered breaths, stiff and uneven as she remained unmoving on the floor. He shut his eyes and tried to massage the headache away before giving in entirely and carefully reaching for the acetaminophen. Shoua's breath stopped, listening intently. Vel gingerly rolled the bottle his way before picking it up. Popping two and swallowing them dry, he grimaced and laid his pounding head against the cool wall. What he wouldn't give for a cigarette—what cigarettes he'd give to see Laura alive again.

"Shoua...," he said weakly, "Before I say sorry, can I ask you something?"

She didn't answer, but the space was his all the same.

"Do you know...Are you on Laura's release forms? From the OB/GYN."

He heard her shift, rubbing what he imagined to be her cheek.

Several times she tried speaking but stopped herself, and when she finally found her voice it was terse and hard—something Vel didn't believe she wanted but the only thing she could actually do in the moment to keep up her own façade.

"Yes. I am. You are, too."

"No," he closed his eyes in pain and shook his head against the wall, "I'm not."

"...*What*," Shoua said, aghast, and finally pulled herself up to sit—albeit away from him, "No, that's bullshit. I was there. She put you on there before me, before her mother."

"They won't release her files to me. Have they released to you?"

"I haven't asked," Shoua thought for a moment, "Do you want me to?"

Vel took his turn thinking, "...No. But you're *sure* I was on there?"

"I watched her struggle with which way the accent on your name should go."

Laura and her lefts and rights. He would've laughed if it weren't so painful.

"One other thing," his eyes stung, "She wasn't...hurt, was she?"

Shoua sucked in a breath.

"She wasn't...raped? Or...,"

"She didn't tell me," Shoua replied, and he felt a very welcome spark of relief, "You don't think...,"

"I don't know," Vel said, wiping his eyes on his shirt, "I don't know, Boots. I don't fucking know anything." Maybe if he was all of what his mother was, or maybe if he had stayed Catholic, or maybe if he had been something whole he would know. But he knew nothing. At this point the fact that he was everything *but* nothing was no longer a saving grace. Inside his pocket the case with his mother's eyes tilted to rest gently against him, but the gesture was lost in his breakdown.

"...I'm sorry, Shoua." Vel dug his fingers between the tendons of his hands because he knew it wasn't enough, "I'm really... really sorry."

Shoua silently turned the flashlight of his phone off and slid it over to him, then to his knowledge in the pitch black, curled away and didn't speak again. Perhaps it was just to cut him off and reject his apology, but part of him felt the shame sink into the room; from her, from him.

12

Somehow, impossibly, Vel *did* sleep. Not very well—his bony ass had not received any kindness from the linoleum floor, his knees were sore, and his head still *pounded*, pounded, desperate for a cigarette he didn't have. And he was cold—in the depths of the summer he was *cold*. For a brief moment he thanked himself for throwing a shirt on and rubbed his neck with a pained whine.

Shoua stirred, though it was unclear if she had previously been awake or not. Without saying a word to him she got up and opened the door, and Vel flinched away from the diffused light of the hallway.

"God," she muttered as she stepped out into her living room, "How am I going to tell my landlord about this?"

Vel tried to stand up and found it to be a multi-step process full of creaks, groans, and complaints as he nursed his ass, back, knees, neck, head. Thirty was only two years away, and he knew he had to get used to it sooner rather than later. Stumbling to the door with half-asleep limbs, he grunted his response.

"Tell 'em it was the flood."

"I want them to *care* about the problem, not ignore it."

Vel laughed, three hoarse croaks that dissolved into a groan of pain and he hid his eyes in his hand. Squeezing his temples in as vice-like a grip as he could manage, he leaned against the frame.

He did not hear Shoua briefly disappear, but did hear her voice turned away from him. She was on the phone, reporting the scene and requesting assistance. Vel could hear the thinly veiled disgust in her voice, then heard his own name drop. When she hung up and tried to pass to the kitchen he mustered a question.

"Me?"

"You know how it is. We're not actively dying, they won't send a car for an hour."

"You're gonna have a pissy cold police lieutenant at your door," he warned weakly.

"Good," Shoua said as she scrounged up cereal, "She'll at least take it seriously."

The cereal clinking into the bowl was agonizing, and Shoua stood in the center of her kitchen to watch him for a moment before softly asking, "Are you okay, Vel?"

"*Cigarette.*" he begged.

"Sorry." she said, quiet to show her sympathy, "Breakfast?"

"What cereal is that?" he grunted, trying to ignore the tingling in his limbs.

"Pure sugar."

"*Fantastic.* That, please."

Shoua filled the bowl with milk before handing it to him and pouring one for herself. Despite her hospitality she was otherwise silent, no doubt thinking of the night before. Vel neither wanted nor was waiting for an apology, but well enough knew that their fight was on her mind. It was on his. He didn't regret it, he didn't think. But also he didn't want to relive it. At least not right away, and it seemed like she was in tacit agreement on that.

The police arrived with little fanfare; a few investigators, a photographer, and Lieu spread out around the house Shoua lived in. One officer took down her statement while Lieu pulled him to the side. He tried telling her what happened in the plainest terms possible, noticing his body was shaking uncontrollably. It was easy to blame it on the lack of nicotine, he wanted to. But the more he relayed, the more he thought about being stuck in the dark with Shoua, exchanging the term *the thing that killed Laura* back and forth until they were screaming and hoarse. It had crawled into his house no louder than a spider, hunting him down while he slept none the wiser. And why? For what? Vel shuddered and tried to rub the tingling out of his arms. The coincidences he had been chasing had led him to a dead end as far as Laura was concerned. Maybe he had dug up *something* viable, but his blind obsession with Laura drove in the complete opposite direction. He had forgotten to be careful. The beast got in his home. *Her* home.

"Vel," Lieu's voice was the same sort of subdued as the day she called him about Laura; the same on a horrific night eleven years ago when she must've decided she would keep him around, "What's the matter with you?"

"Cigarette," he begged again, "I can't think."

Lieu frowned, "Let me ask."

Luckily for him, one of her officers did have a pack on them. Different than his regular brand but god he would go for anything, even a piece of gum. After he had a few drags, Lieu asked him to recount it again. He did. A little clearer—not by much, but the more he relaxed into the smoke the better he felt, the more he described. Lieu wrote it down; she always wrote down what he said no matter how insane, and by her sigh at the end he knew it *did* sound insane.

But the marks were hard to deny. With the nicotine back in his body Vel looked at the shredded remains of Shoua's door, the bestial slashes across the window frames, the claw marks in the decorative rocks. Yet the other side of her door, still graced with the willowspine wreath, looked untouched. It bent with the sway of the willow branch that knew better than to try and withstand the wind, it stood firm with the stubborn strength of a boar to weather the worst. Something moved in his pocket to tap him for attention, but he ignored it.

He released a sigh, dropped the cigarette on the ground, and stopped.

"Oh." he said dumbly, looking at his bare foot. He had borrowed a pair of Shoua's sandals, not to wear but to stand on the pavement that was already blistering temperatures (if the tips of his toes reaching far beyond Shoua's small shoe size gave him any indication). Lieu wordlessly reached and snuffed it for him.

"Anything else?"

Tap tap. Hell, her eyes were going ballistic in his pocket!

"Not at the moment, no." Vel answered truthfully. Well. He hadn't told Lieu about all the investigating he was doing on the side, but. Y'know. Not relevant. He pulled his phone out and waited for the screen to adjust to the morning light, groaning when 7:30am stared back at him. Now, he had thought doing that would settle the issue by giving her eyes room to breathe, but it was insistent against his thigh. It was more physical than audible, impatient *tap, tap, tapping* that increasingly became hard to ignore.

"Are you going home?"

Tap tap.

"If I stay a moment longer than needed Shoua'll kill me," *tap tap*, god damn it, he was tapping his foot against the sandals to mask it lest it was visible to Lieu and prompted the awkwardest question ever between them, "Hey, can I bum another cig for the road?"

The second Lieu left he stuffed his hand in his pocket. Okay, okay, he got the message, *okay!* Vel bit his lip, hoping he looked somewhat normal as he took the cigarette. Or at least that he looked like he needed to piss, because that would at least be a considerably normal explanation. Regardless he turned away from everyone to give them space from the smoke—that was the idea, anyway. (He had to stick his fuckoff big feet in Shoua's tiny little sandals to walk, and even just using the balls of his feet did not make them fit any better.)

His mother's eyes were precious to him for more than one reason. Yes, it was a never-decaying gift from her bloodied hand, her last ditch effort to protect him at great cost. A *gift*. Rarely did he indulge in the gift; there was something so spiritual about their air that they spooked him. As such, there was no way in hell he could use them for personal gain. His mother never raised a chancla like his tía did, but misusing her eyes would have her find a way to do that from beyond the grave. That was the simplest way he figured it.

When they were practically trying to bounce out of their case, however, that was another story. They were still in some part his mother, and a mother like her only ever did everything to protect her son. No—in life she had never been fickle with her power when it came to him. With a glance around to make sure everyone's focus was elsewhere, Vel slipped the cigarette between two fingers and pulled the case open just enough to take one out. Laying his tongue flat, he placed the eyeball in his mouth, parted his lips, and used his tongue to help adjust until she faced outward. All the while he kept the cigarette poised to mimic the act of smoking, hiding her from untoward sight.

Vel breathed through his nose and faced Shoua's apartment, letting himself see with his mother's gaze. It took some adjusting—it always did, like putting on a viewfinder's image over what his eyes were already seeing. After a long night of stress and withdrawal he felt so dizzy he might throw up, but pressing his tongue to the roof of his mouth helped while his lips held the eye. He blinked back stinging tears, relaxed, and allowed his regular vision to lose focus while his mother's eye filled in for him.

The bestial scratch marks warped and disappeared, replaced instead by deep cleaving gashes. Even near the window there was a semi-circle impression in the frame that was from a blunt force swing, not a digging claw.

The cigarette went slack in his fingers. The eye had to fill in the space in his thoughts for him too, and when it did the word couldn't stop echoing in his head. *Axe. Axe marks.*

That was the truth of the matter, magic and smoke stripped bare. Vel retched, doubling over and popping the eye into his palm. People glanced over and he closed his hand, summoning the deep and throaty smoker's cough to answer their question. A few more coughs to recover (a little more real than he wanted them to be, but it helped the act) and he put the eye back with its sister. Vel then lit the cigarette proper and returned the officer's lighter.

Axe marks.

Laura's killer *was* the same as the others. Moreover, the killer knew who he was and targeted him, likely for getting too close. In his pocket the eyes had stilled back into inanimate objects, having shown him what they wanted.

His mind bloomed to life, not quite putting the details together yet but finally being in the *state* to do so. It was elating, having not felt this since, well, since she had died. A sort of break in the fog. He wasn't through it yet but he was *going* to be.

His eyes suddenly fell on Shoua, holding her elbows while she watched the officers finish taking their notes. Immediately he wanted to confirm her suspicions, she was right, they were both right, Laura was *murdered*. Without thinking he stumbled forward in her sandals, making it halfway before his racing mind slowed him down to mind two things. One, Lieu was enough in earshot to be suspicious.

Two, if the creature, the killer, had any cognizance about it, it now knew where Shoua lived too—and if nothing else, that Vel trusted her enough to shelter in her place. It didn't take a genius to derive that she was in danger.

"Hey," the cigarette bounced in his lips as he spoke and reached to herd her away from the front of the building, "Can I talk to you for a sec?"

Shoua didn't say yes but she didn't exactly say no either, following him to the shady side of the split-level house. Her elbows remained firmly secure in her grasp and she sighed, looking at everywhere except him.

"You alright?" he asked.

"This is my 2am, I'm tired." she grumbled back. After a bit she finally flicked her eyes over, albeit just staring at his chest. With a playfully disgusted scowl she asked, "What even are you wearing?"

"You only just noticed?" he pouted, the cigarette pushing out and down. Vel stretched out the sleep shirt so she could better see it for its glory—the faded and crumbling ink, the hole in the collar, the tea stains he couldn't get out of the rough cotton fabric, the severe and smug faces of Looney Tunes characters dressed in the uniforms of the Phoenix Suns—Vel glanced up at her and grinned, "It's a classic."

"How *long* have you had that?"

"Mom found it in a yard sale when I was, uh, four, I think—guess someone decided to be a Bulls fan instead."

Shoua's nose wrinkled, "Spare me the details on what you've done in that thing."

Vel wasted no time in lifting his arm against the side of the building, mimicking a too-cool-for-school punk while *also* giving her the full view of the hair in his armpit, visible from the hole that had eaten up half the seam on that side. That got Shoua to meet his eyes *specifically* to glare at him, and he only grinned wider.

"What did I *just* fucking say."

"Hey now," he took a drag of the cigarette as his voice softened, "I could tell you about how my mom swaddled me in this shirt when it was longer than my body. I was small once, y'know."

Shoua shut her eyes, likely trying to force the image from her mind as if she was in no state to express emotion responsibly. Vel didn't expect it of her. She took in a shaky breath and asked, "What do you want?"

"Are you alright?" He didn't break his gaze as he turned his head to the side to blow the smoke away from her.

"You *asked* me that already," Shoua's voice was hard, but he still heard the precarious twang of annoyance in her words.

"I know," Vel said, "It's important."

"I'm—," she began, frustration from the previous night bubbling back up, "No, it's none of your business, actually, okay?"

"Sorry Boots, but I've already *made* it my business," Vel put the cigarette back in his lips, "You could be in danger now."

"And I have *you* to thank for it," she harshly reminded him. For once he didn't flinch.

"I know. Have you talked to someone? Anyone?"

"About last night? Vel—,"

"About Laura," he interrupted, "About everything. Including my fuck-ups."

Stunned, Shoua's face grappled with deep anger and potent fear, floundering in front of him as choked little sounds escaped her throat.

"I know it can't be me," Vel said gently, "But I worry about you."

"*Don't*," she croaked, "Oh my god, *don't*, not from *you*."

"C'mon, Boots," he argued, his voice still soft but getting exasperated, "I don't care who it is. *Somebody*."

"Just leave me—," Shoua stopped mid-sentence, let out a frustrated growl that didn't do enough to cover up the hurt, and tried to bolt. Vel caught her quick and pulled her flat against his chest (well, she barely came to the bottom of his chest but it didn't matter), once again holding tight. Vel held the cigarette at an angle away from her so he wouldn't accidentally ash on her skin. It wasn't quite against his *better* judgment but certainly it was against some judgment. Shoua struggled, clawing at his shirt and kicking at his shins. (Thank god she was not *actually* wearing her boots.)

"I hate you," she growled into his shirt, "I *hate* you!!"

"Yeah I know." he pitched forward to puff delicately. She was going to say more, actually kill him like he knew she would, but just as she was about to break free Lieu approached them. At the sound of someone else being present, Shoua froze and pressed her face harder against Vel, hiding.

Lieu gave a clinical rundown of what she planned to do with the report, although results weren't promising. Vel answered as though there wasn't someone plastered in his hold against her will. Once she advised that he go home to wrap this up, she looked at Shoua. Far be it from her to extend warmth, she simply flipped her notebook closed and trusted Vel to be safe. He watched her go, knowing he elected not to tell Lieu what he actually suspected now that he had seen what the claw marks actually were. That may have been a stupid idea, but at this point Lieu would only get in the way.

"Shoua I don't think...," he started as Lieu got into her car, "I don't think it's good to see each other for a bit."

Shoua nodded vigorously against him. No arguments. No snarky remarks. It was simply the best suggestion he had made since the funeral.

"I think you should keep the wreath on your door for now. I'll come pick it up when it's all over." Finally he loosened his grip, took the last drag, and pulled away from her. She avoided his gaze again, this time with prejudice—but with the officers gone she curiously did not rush to flee from him back to her apartment.

"I *do* care about you, Boots," he was going to leave it at that but the half-drunk memory of her couch zapped him and he added, "As a friend. No weird stuff."

He dropped the cigarette, lifted his foot, gave a quiet scoff, and did a few odd stomps with Shoua's sandal to snuff it out. She watched. If he didn't know any better he might've guessed she was downright transfixed.

"Gonna make a break for it. Call me if it gets really bad. Please."

Before Shoua could ask, counter, or jeer, Vel turned and

wobble-walked to his car. The worst was when he had to leave Shoua's sandals at the curb, and he pinched his lips between grit teeth as he skittered around to the driver's side. His soles may have been thick but the desert sun was unforgiving. At the *very* least he had not encountered any rattlers throughout the whole ordeal. As he started his car and winced at the heat of the pedals, he swore to himself that he was going to get a pair of sandals for his bedroom in case this happened again. Anything to ignore that Shoua was watching him leave.

13

He impatiently tapped the steering wheel the entire drive home. He didn't tell Shoua not to stop for strangers *or* familiar faces on the side of the road. Sure, she had said she wasn't likely to do that, even for him, but, but, *but.*

Every woman had known the killer—the beast, however that happened. He must've flagged them down on the road likely late at night, pretending to have car troubles. Every woman stopped to help, every woman was slaughtered in his car, then driven away to be dumped. Vel tapped the wheel harder. Their abdomens, or perhaps more accurately their genitals, had been mutilated—even with Laura's exemption her face had largely remained untouched as opposed to the lower portions of her body. He was sure they had all been pregnant—three out of five from the same clinic was no coincidence anymore. At that same clinic, there had been a truck with smudged fingerprints on the hood—many of them. He wanted to kick himself. If he hadn't been needing a cigarette at the time, if he had given it some thought, he would've liked to have looked at the bed and tried to figure if there had been any blood, even if he had to smell for it.

He couldn't be sure it was Dr. Thompson just yet based on feeling alone. If he had been in his shoes, meeting an angry distraught boyfriend in that sort of clinic...yeah Vel would not have been as accommodating even if he was trying to de-escalate. Lieu was right, the case was hurting him and thusly hurting his ability to investigate cleanly.

Now of course, that didn't mean that he should've followed her orders. He was so close, no one could tell him otherwise.

Or rather, it was so close to *him*. At this point he didn't have a choice.

His phone blared to life, thankfully not with Lieu's ring-tone. No, just the usual Owl City song that Shoua, metalhead, would've given him shit for if the call was twenty minutes earlier. Vel slowed turning onto his street, grabbing his phone to answer.

It was Jean Benoit. Vel pushed the phone into the crook of his shoulder.

"Sorry it took me a while," Jean said, "I asked after you called but there was a problem—they didn't get back to me until they were just about to close."

"No, this turnaround is fantastic," Vel said, alert despite the lack of sleep, "What do you mean problem?"

"Well—," Jean paused. Vel egged him on, noting that nothing was unimportant especially at this point. Finally a hint of frustration crept into his voice, and with it, more of the French Bayou accent he hid, "...They said I wasn't on her release forms."

Thank god he was already pulling into his driveway because Vel slammed on the brakes so suddenly he lurched forward in his seat, "*What.*"

"Nah, nah, I *should've* been on her release forms. I was there with her," Jean swallowed, "I swear I was."

"Yeah, no, it—," Vel bit back the snarl and eased his car into the garage and shut it off, "Sorry, then what?"

"Well they turned me away until about, five? They called me back yeah, and said there had been a mix-up. How the hell? I don't know. But they sent me the stuff anyway."

Vel paused, "That *seems* quick. Actually—it doesn't matter. What was the name of Chelsea's doctor?"

Jean answered, "Dr. Randall Thompson."

Vel stared at the wall of his garage, cold and angry. Taking in a deep breath to remain professional, Vel then clarified, "So you called immediately after I hung up?"

"Yeah, otherwise I work past the time they're open."

"And they sent it around five?"

"Yeah exactly."

In-between that time Vel had shown up and raised a little hell, revealing to Dr. Thompson that he was not only an investigator but one that might've been getting close enough to rattle the cages. So...if both his and Jean's names had been erased from the forms, but it was discovered that Chelsea had been *married* and not just a girlfriend, a cornered killer acting out of fear might've restored Jean's name to the documents and released them. It would've taken time and Vel had no doubt he had appointments to attend to. A last ditch effort as the doors close to save ass.

"Detective Velasquez...?"

"Vel—just Vel, that's fine," he shook his head. He wanted very badly to scream in the phone, share his anger and frustration that his name should've been on there too, Laura's records should be in his hand too—he didn't know why they were both erased, he couldn't fathom it. He wanted to scream that it was *unfair*, so goddamn unfair and stupid and this should've never have happened, right, Jean? He should have a wife with a round belly and a finished degree, should move back to Louisiana and teach his kid Creole, and Vel should have that too. Vel should be getting his shit together right about now and discuss with Laura whether or not they wanted to get married or just stay life partners without the certificate. It wouldn't matter to him, he was certain he'd still have Laura forever, if he could've, if the world was fair. Vel grit his teeth and uttered, "I can't— Thank you, Jean. I can't tell you quite yet but you've been. Very helpful."

"Appreciate it," Jean said, though it was clear he had caught on to Vel's personal torment, "Need anything else?"

"No—well. Are you staying in town?"

"Do I need to?" Jean's voice perked in suspicion.

"No, no no, I don't think so," Besides, he had his number if he truly needed it, "I just wanted to know."

Jean was silent for a moment before answering, "...I'm going to take a break. Finish my degree later. Or...I don't know. I miss home. Shoulda listened to Mawmaw and stayed closer."

Vel rubbed his eyes to avoid looking at the home he was about to enter and tried to joke, "Well, if it makes you feel any better, I *did* stay home." With a dry and pained laugh, he pulled the phone away from his face, "I'll contact you soon, hopefully with good news."

He was going to pay another visit to the clinic, this time with suspicions of misconduct under his arm. Prove that, and the killer—the beast—might show again. He had to get at the files, and with the smoke and mirrors already present in the clinic, he was going to have to sneak his way in.

Vel felt the weight of the case push him down as he entered his—Laura's—home. That, paired with the absolute dogshit way he slept half the night, and Vel was ready to pass out. In fact, that was going to be the best idea for his plan.

First, though, the spare bedroom's door was splintered into the hallway and the room proper. Upon peering inside, he noticed that the window was for the *most* part untouched. Another curiosity, but instead of fretting about it he simply slid the window shut over the slashed screen and picked his way back to his bed to sleep.

* * *

He woke up again, groggy, feeling the house rumble with thunder—no, footsteps. Footsteps and hot-cool wind whipping through the valley. He sat up in bed and rubbed his eyes, finding it harder than usual to clear them of sleep.

"Laura?"

She had been so late to get home and hadn't texted him what the holdup was. But he had gone to sleep before to wake up with her, it wasn't uncalled for, it was fine that he fell asleep. Right?

No, something wasn't right. He felt it in his gut, he was forgetting something. His eyes swept to the empty crib and then to the coyote tail out the door.

Vel shouted, springing to his feet and running. He was barefoot, he was fully dressed, he was naked and still warm from Laura's embrace, his feet stung on the hot rocks. It was night and the breeze warned of a coming storm, but still he ran, pursuing the coyote to the edges of the city and the foothills of Mica Mountain. Splashes of Mexican color struggled from the coyotes mouth. It glanced back at him, its gaze feral and intelligent, taunting and hungry. The mound in the sarape smacked against rock; Vel scrambled up the crumbling foothill until he could grasp the coyote's tail and yank.

The coyote released the sarape in a howling flash of teeth and pain, and Vel dropped the tail to reach for what was inside. It hit him like a truck, much bigger than he had supposed, and by the time he recognized it as Laura the coyote had closed its fangs around the head of his child.

He heard the screams of a name he had never had the chance to say in childhood. The child a baby, two years old, older with the long scrawny limbs they inherited from Vel flailing. Vel reached into the jaws of the coyote but wrenched nothing but blood away. He staggered backwards, haunted by how his hands glistened black in the moonlight despite the lack of a moon in the sky.

Vel's long limbs tripped over Laura's body in his baby blanket, a bright pink and colorful sarape that his mother had wrapped around herself for warmth when she crossed the border. The pink was stained black in the night and he panicked. Hands slipping on the blood, Vel uncovered her face—pale and untouched. But he felt it, felt how her body moved awkward and distorted, chewed apart from the waist down.

"Laura?" he pet back her dry hair, blood from the coyote's mouth clotting in her strands, "Laura I'm sorry,"

"Jeró?" she muttered sweetly, as though she was just getting out of bed. Laura smiled at him and reached a hand to his cheek, brushing her knuckles along the barbed frizz at his jaw, "Did tortillas ever puff up for you?"

"What does it matter," he choked, "I love you. I want to stay. I want you to stay."

"How far can a mouse run, Jeró?"

"Huh?" he was sobbing, confused and grasping at something he was only just now remembering he no longer had.

The same rumbling footsteps that had been in his house broke against the rocks and Vel looked up. The coyote was big, bigger, shaggy and nondescript in its shape. Bison-like shoulders, moved like a cat, almost a man, and in its jaws a river of blood. "How far?"

Vel held Laura closer, watching the beast approach with claw-tipped hands. Closer still, then he ducked his head around her as the last breaths left her body and the beast snapped forward. *How far can a mouse run?*

14

There was something liminally uncanny about the clinic in the dead dark of night. It was a place that was built to be seen not just in the daytime, but in the brightest Arizona sun. Moreover, the pavement was wet from the midday storms that Vel had slept through. A moist smell warmed the air, leftover from the rain that had turned to steam upon hitting the pavement. Vel had circled the clinic earlier, getting two meals from the nearby mall and sitting to scout at the end of their operating hours. The front double doors were used the most and were guarded by a domed security camera. When the janitor left for the night he noted the pause in movement near the door and figured a numpad-based system as well.

After that, he had gone home and raided his supplies before returning hours later. Tucson fell asleep around him, but he was wired.

How far can a mouse run, Jeró?

He shoveled the last of the mall's chicken teriyaki in his mouth, trying to push down the question. Sickened by the dream, when he awoke he dressed himself in a wooden rosary and his bracelet of saints. He ran his fingers over the beads while he waited, sometimes saying a Hail Mary, most times with prayers muttered in the back of his mind but not at the

137

forefront. More time passed, and he finally felt it dead enough to move.

First, the camera. Off to the side Vel pulled out a sheet of clear cellophane and smoothed it against the building's wall. They did not have the *friendliest* security cameras for someone looking to break in because this was Tucson and they knew better. Still Vel smoothed it until it was as flat as it could be, and tucked his way beneath the domed camera at the front. Whether or not he was captured on film was...Well, he was sure he'd find out eventually. Eyeballing the measurements, he used a backup jackknife to cut slits until he could mimic the dome shape and lightly taped the edges closed. (His original, with its beads and cords wrapped around the hilt, was still stuck in Shoua's door.) Then he stole back out of the view of the camera and re-laid the cellophane flat.

Vel judged the eye of the camera and what it saw. It was going to be a messy job but for one night in and out it should work—even if the camera recorded in color. Pulling out his phone he took the best approximation of the camera's reach that he could, thankful for his height for once. Ducking away, he messed with both the contrast of the photo until it was as high as it could possibly be and flipped it to a negative. Once the brightness was turned up, he pocketed his phone.

At the very least, the bushes around the building were already budding with greenery because the next part had to be as far in the dark as he could make it. Vel pulled out a bottle of gelatin emulsified with silver nitrate that he kept in a black pouch and a flat paint brush. Relaxing his eyes as much as possible to see into the night, he painted the mixture onto the cellophane. He had mixed the emulsifier himself about a year ago when a client was tangled in a discrepancy over family history, their ancestor appearing in the negatives but never in the actual photographs developed. Back then it had taken three tries and a frustrated prayer, here he only had the grace for one. Vel pulled out the sharpest mint gum he could find at the corner store and chewed two at once. At the peak of its flavor, he carefully blew the chill onto the solidifying emulsifier.

Now, the hard part. With the emulsifier cooled so that it became a makeshift glass pane, Vel carefully touched the branches of the nearby plants.

"Could you hold this straight for a sec?" he asked, lifting the cellophane pane until it rested between two opposing branches, "Like this. Good rain we're having, right? You already look beautiful." He waited until the plants brushed and curled around the cellophane in curiosity before letting go.

"Thanks. No dirty doings on my end, promise. And I got what I'm about to do from California, some eight hours up the road. You ever been?" Vel chatted with them as he dug into his backpack and pulled out a vial of borax, carefully harvested from seasonal dry lakes. It would work with artificial borax, sure—but it was a better bet this way and even just mentioning how he got it made the plants hold the cellophane firmer than before.

"No one talks to you much, huh?" his phone was next, "But I bet you hear a whole lot. Hold still, please." Vel tucked the long tail of the rosary's cross into his lips, clamping down and praying hard. One, two—he flashed the negative image of the camera's view point for five seconds then shut his phone off.

"Perfect, hold it, and," Vel untwisted the cap of the natural borax and brushed it on the emulsified pane, then sat back on his ass, "We wait."

Of course, not without conversation, even if his voice was

hampered by both the gum and the crucifix in his mouth, "Did you ever see a woman come 'round here? Late twenties, blonde hair, blue eyes—she came up to my chest, thereabouts. Might've come in with someone shorter than her, otherwise alone."

He paused, conjuring an image of Laura in his mind and finding he couldn't find better ways to describe her without going down a hole, "...I miss her. Y'know. That's why I was here the other day."

Vel peered into the darkness, seeing shapes form on the cellophane. He'd give it 30 seconds more, but he had to guess rather than use his phone.

"You could say that's a reason I'm here now, too." his voice took a somber turn. The plants were quiet and he counted out the rest of the wait in his head before he dug the gum out of his mouth. With the other hand he gently took the photo away and shook off the borax solution on the pavement, as he didn't know if the plants appreciated the mineral. They took the photo back into their hold without complaint, at least. Splitting the gum into four mostly-even clumps, he attached one to each corner of the cellophane. Gum, sticky and cold to slow the development. At least it smelled nicer than stop bath solution. Vel picked on a scab he had gotten from rescuing Emily and pressed it into one of the pieces of gum. Blood, coagulated and stopped, to seal the deal. Finally, the most important item to have on any excursion be it one of Vel's weird witcheries or the outdoors in general: A water bottle. Running water washed everything off magic or otherwise.

He lifted the makeshift photo to the light and squinted. Looked like a shitty security camera feed to him! Smiling in triumph, Vel concluded his conversation with the plants as he pulled a sheet of parchment paper equal in size to the cellophane to act as backing.

"Well, I'll let you know how it goes. Sometimes you just get a feeling, y'know? I'll say hi on my way out." Locating the slits in the cellophane, Vel re-cut and re-did the dome and placed it over the security camera, sticking it with the gum.

From there it was a breeze. His jiggler lock pick made quick work of the front door and he slipped in. One long stride to the numpad. A tube of glitter was already in his hand, leftover from Laura's exuberance in Renaissance Faires and other art markets. He was counting on its significance—the memory of Laura stepping once more into this clinic—when he poured a mound into his hand and blew it onto the numpad. From the thickest layer of glitter to the least, he punched in 3750 and held his breath.

It stuck, and the alarm disarmed. Vel sighed in relief. At the very least he was impressed that the code wasn't *obviously* a birthday. He took a moment to lean against the wall, catching his thoughts and slowing down. He wasn't...*exactly* proficient at break-ins. Or at least that's what he told Lieu whenever he whipped out the ring of lock pick keys. Every building was different, from the land to the people (or the plants!) the building was used to seeing. Therefore every approach had to be different.

But now that he was in, unless there were other surprises, he should be good to go until he had to extract himself. He had not *quite* planned for how to cover his tracks, but he rarely planned for every step anyway. Contingencies could only be accounted for when there was a finite number, and in his experience there *was* no finite number. Too many fuck-ups as an arrogant teenager taught him that.

Vel finally let go of the crucifix and pulled the small flashlight from his backpack to tuck between his teeth instead. Before zipping it back up he took his phone and typed out the address of where he was and why to Lieu. Didn't hit send, of course, but just in case shit went sideways. It might not save him but it'd help Lieu figure out what the hell he was up to in his last moments.

Now. He shined the light into the lobby and retraced his steps to the examination room Dr. Thompson had taken him to. Vel flinched at the ghastly brightness of the metal stirrups that cast crooked shadows on the wall. Turning his attention quickly to the cabinets he picked each locked one but only found medical supplies. Cussing, he closed them and double-checked their lock before turning around in the room. Nothing else. So he crept back out into the hall, shining the light up and down. Vel squinted. There were more doors tucked beyond the examination rooms, and upon closer inspection he saw nameplates on the outside. So there *were* offices. Thompson had just been fucking with him. A quick jiggle-pick later and he was in.

There they all were. File cabinets and a computer both. Vel leaned over the desk to turn the computer on, figuring he'd check the actual paper files while he waited for it to boot up. While there he lightly brushed his fingers along the underside of the desk, hissing when they came across a plastic box. Panic button. Vel gingerly flicked it open to expose the button—again, just in case—and turned to the cabinets.

Jiggle, open. He sifted through until he pulled Laura's file and placed it on the desk. Flashlight in mouth, he opened the folder and there was her handwriting. Gently, Vel spread the sheets out to look at them in totality. Nothing looked out of place, the address, allergens, and personal information all worked out.

But on the release form, she had seemingly skipped a box before filling out her mother's name. Then Shoua's. Vel rubbed his thumb over the dried whiteout. Anger rose in him, pain and anger that made his lips snarl over the flashlight. He could hurt something. *Person removed under patient's request. RT.*

Bullshit. *Bullshit.* Tears of frustration burned his eyes. He couldn't even see where Laura undoubtedly scratched out the first O in his name to rewrite it with the properly leaning accent.

Vel whipped back to the cabinets. Jiggle, open, jiggle, open. He pulled Chelsea Benoit's file, then, seeing it nearby, Diana Berkeley's. Then the two other women. Everyone but Chelsea's had been the same: whited out names where their partner's presumably were. Chelsea's was the only one with Jean listed, but Vel recognized the handwriting where he shouldn't have—Thompson's, no doubt refilled in a panic after Vel had stirred the pot.

Vel bit down on a knuckle to stifle his rage. It had to be Thompson. If not the murderer he was severing ties between couples—couples that felt too specific to feel comfortable. There were several reasons to pick an OB/GYN carefully, Vel knew, but one so rotten had still slipped through into a clinic that had otherwise good reviews. Good enough that Laura trusted them. Good enough that Emily was able to have a next-day appointment to ensure her baby's safety.

He stuck the flashlight back in his mouth. When and where the rot started wasn't mattering to him in the moment. He had to pile the papers up into one folder, slip them in his pack, and get out. It'd take far too much convincing Lieu but he was about to do it, already scripting excuses and what he needed to say in order to force a warrant.

He was seconds away from flipping the folder closed when a key turned in the door and it opened. Laura's pendant in his pocket turned to bite into his leg. Vel stood, frozen in the reach of his flashlight. Dr. Thompson entered.

"Well," Thompson greeted cordially. Vel dropped the flashlight into his hand and held it just beneath the good doctor's face, "I figured you might be here."

Vel swallowed, having not expected to speak to anyone tonight, "How so?"

"It's so late, and you weren't at home!" Thompson answered, approaching the chair on the opposite side of the desk, "Finding you at a bar was a long shot, why not start here?"

Vel turned his thumb and closed the file. Thompson watched, an odd non-smile smile on his lips as he tilted his head.

"I'll uh, save you the trouble. There's really only a bar or two I go to. And not so much recently." Laura enjoyed seeing Shoua at work, and the three of them frequented a different bar for karaoke night. It was mostly for his and Laura's sake and Shoua's relaxation; the two of them taking turns singing wantonly. Vel would get into it, heat from the energy of the song warming him while Laura watched with eager glee.

Heat was starting to warm him now but for entirely different reasons, and while Thompson's eyes were a similar shade of blue the eagerness in them was not so loving.

"But you're not gonna tell me, are you?" Thompson guessed.

Vel slid the file away from his hand creeping along the desk,

"Nope."

"I suppose you have questions," he was posturing with the calmness of his voice, "You can ask away."

Vel was the opposite of calm, and already he felt that as jaws ensnaring his body. Thompson was expecting that, expecting his rage and sorrow and fear to drive him. The more crazed Vel looked or acted, the more Thompson reported his break-in with wine-smooth talk, the less Vel legitimized himself. He had *been* that crazy Mexican kid shouting behind bars. Had it not been for Lieu, he wouldn't have been listened to at all.

So, Vel swallowed again and tried to wet his quickly drying mouth, "I don't know if I do, actually. I don't think it matters."

"Oh, come on," Thompson *tsked* in teasing disappointment, "What kind of private investigator are you?"

"I look for clues," Vel replied pointedly, "Not answers."

"Y'know as a doctor I can respect that angle, but also as a doctor I know your head doesn't work that way," Thompson pointed at the space between his eyes and Vel furrowed his brow, so tense he felt Thompson's finger on placebo alone. So what if he was right? Vel didn't want to back down and *show* that he had been, "So what clues have you found?"

"Enough," Vel said, guarded, "Evidence you've been tampering with patient files, likely digitally too."

Thompson raised his eyebrows, "You're going for a malpractice suit?"

Vel stared, silent. "Actually, I do have a question. Why did you drive by my house?"

"Call it...," Thompson was at the corner of the desk now, and Vel had backed to the opposite end, "A little bit of benevolent malpractice. For the sake of the clinic."

"I don't think—," Vel slipped the file off of the desk proper and tapped it to have the little sound fill the dark room, "—that I'm quite your type."

"And what type would that be?"

Bastard was trying to make Vel say the quiet parts out loud. Vel ground his teeth and took the bait, "White women. With not-so-white partners."

"Is *that* what you think," Thompson laughed, ridiculing him, "This city is full of interracial relationships, what makes you so sure?"

"Hunches got me this far," he narrowed his eyes.

"Aren't you reading into it a little much? I'm no racist," Thompson explained just as calm as he had been this whole time, and Vel's guts twisted into a fist he wish he could use, "If it makes you feel any better, at least they won't be abandoned and impoverished once the baby is born."

A flash of red hit Vel and his control fractured at the edges. Raging heat rose to his face and trembling fingers. His vision blurred and the saliva in his mouth had a tangy taste when he spat out, "Laura was a *realtor*."

Thompson stopped, and regardless—or perhaps oblivious to this—Vel continued, the angry words tumbling without end.

"She *found* that house. She bought it *with me*, for the *both of us*," he seethed, "Her name was *first* on the mortgage. It's *hers*," *more hers than it'll ever be his.*

Vel's shoulders heaved up and down, jolting when Thompson spoke again.

"A miscalculation, then. Doctors can't be right all the time, we're only human. But I did some detective work myself. Where is your father, Mr. Velasquez—and is that your mother's name?"

Never before had Vel been so close to dropping everything just to wrap his hands around someone's neck. Thompson knew it, too. The pendant in his pocket was trembling to a beat he didn't recognize. All it was doing was reminding him more and more of Laura and more and more of what he lost to the man in front of him.

"You're a man of faith, aren't you?" Thompson asked, and in his haze Vel didn't understand what he meant until he gestured to the rosary around his neck, "Surely you know that revenge isn't the way of things."

"And what? Leave myself to your mercy?" Vel growled, backing away as Thompson approached, "I don't really trust you came here to let me live."

Thompson laughed a little and said, "Well, you don't have the best intentions either, do you?"

Vel's back was to the door that left the office, but there wasn't enough space for him to make it before Thompson caught up with him. His tía's voice recited scriptures in his mind, distracting him as well as acting as a mantra. What part of the Bible was it? Something to do with San Paulo.

"So what's it gonna be then? Axe in your truckbed?"

Thompson laughed harder, "I'm not an idiot. In fact killing you here will drive the police off any scent you might've given them."

"Don't be so sure," it was the first time he felt he had the upper hand in the entire confrontation. Thompson narrowed his eyes, but Vel dove, startling him backward as he used his long reach over the desk to press the panic button. Then he challenged, "Make it quick."

Thompson scowled, and from his back pocket a heavy iron meat pounder emerged. Vel couldn't run—even a missed throw from that could break a bone or badly trip him, and he wasn't so sure the adrenaline would cover it up. Plus, there were other things that he was banking on working that likely wouldn't; if the TPD showed up on time (fat chance) Thompson would *hopefully* not have killed him. But since he couldn't trust that, he had to last Thompson out—and by the time they *did* arrive Vel would have to convince them that *he* was the victim despite breaking and entering Thompson's workplace. He had gambled himself into a losing battle, but taking such a harsh chance had at least put Thompson on the back-step.

No matter what happened at this point, he was going to wind up the crazy Mexican behind bars again—only this time he was a fully legal adult, and Lieu would likely not or be unable to save him.

The pendant was going wild and as soon as Thompson lurched into a threatening stance something made him choke. Vel started, both hands going into his pockets—retrieving the pendant to pretend that was his goal while his other hand sent the prepared message to Lieu. When the pendant emerged Thompson retched, sweat beading on his skin. It stunned Vel to silence where he was originally going to demand if Thompson recognized it.

"*Ah...you...,*" Thompson struggled, and Vel, really not knowing what was going on, could only watch dumbly as the good doctor splayed against the desk and coughed, his eyes rimmed in red, "You and your girlfriend...Something's different about you two...,"

"Yeah?" Vel asked, stalling, "What?"

"Feel...*powerful*...," Thompson hacked and spat saliva, "Strong. Hungry," his voice dissolved into a thunderous groan as the veins popped on his skin. Thompson looked up at Vel, holding the wildly swinging pendant in front of him, "Makes me feel good. Makes *it* feel good."

Vel stumbled back and Thompson clamped his hand on the edge of the desk. His fingers went white with pressure against the plastic-covered wood, then jutted into the desk, splintering it in his hand.

"Felt it near your house...In your house...Felt it near *her*. And I tore, and tore, and *tore* and it was *delicious*,"

"The *fuck...*," Vel sputtered, suddenly hearing and seeing a different man in front of him. Well, for as long as he stayed a man. The thought jolted him suddenly, and his eyes flicked to the pendant as Thompson writhed and raked his nails against his clothes.

"Feels like I was chosen. Feels like God wants it," Thompson sputtered, blood spattering from his mouth as his insides crunched and stretched, "What do you think, man of faith?"

Vel's mind raced. His mother had once told him of a tale of transformation, but he never understood it as something she could do *willfully*. Transformation seemed far-fetched, a fairy tale trait of monsters, liars, and curses. But here, Laura's pendant seemed to will Dr. Thompson into something heinous and bestial. There was no time to untangle *why*, all he knew was a newfound streak of desperate rage was sweeping over him. He had made the pendant to *protect* her, not seal her fate. He had used a mouse's rib to *escape from danger*—

Thompson tried to compose himself, closing his hand again on the meat pounder.

—else she landed in the jaws of it.

With the rage came a stinging sense of determination. His eyes stung with hot, pained tears, betrayed not from the uselessness of his witchcraft but in that it worked too well. Vel tightened his hand, pulling the pendant up into his palm. By now he had gambled all his fucks away and accepted he wasn't walking out of this a free man, much less alive. If the pendant truly was going to be an escape from danger as he originally imagined it, if the pendant had served him well simply because of Laura's imprinted memory of terror and care, then it would serve him once more.

Romans, chapter 12 verse 20. *If your enemy is hungry, feed him; for by doing so you will heap burning coals upon his head.*

Vel yanked the pendant free from the cord then lunged forward and struck Thompson across the cheek. Spittle flew from his loosened jaw. Snatching it and holding his mouth open, Vel clapped the pendant into Thompson's mouth and clamped down, willing him to swallow. Thompson's bloodshot eyes went wide, glaring at him in rage that turned more and more bestial by the second. Then, in the violent roiling of his muscles, he swallowed and Vel pushed away.

Thompson laughed, an ugly triumphant sound that shredded the edges of his voice until it was in total distortion. Vel saw his body rip and tear itself apart, but fled out the door before he saw the end of the beast's transformation. A horrible roar cut over the sound of breaking flesh and bone, and Vel yelped when the roar crashed through into the hallway behind him.

His boots skidded into the back of the lobby and he had to paw at the floor with his hands to recover his balance. The front doors glowed with the yellow porchlight outside, but the tremors from the steps of the beast were on his heels. A straight shot would kill him for sure. Vel ducked behind the receptionist's desk just as the beast's feet left the floor, watching it crash into the waiting room chairs in horror. Vel stood at full height, eyes wide, body frozen.

Of that single story of transformation his mother had, she

had described being turned into the body of a jackrabbit—long-limbed, nimble, hunted, the perfect statue until it was time to run. The beast turned, whipping the remnants of a chair from its head, and locked eyes on him. Vel stayed, watched the beast approach, break into a run, leap for his head.

Vel dove under the desk. It would've worked had it not been for his ridiculous height as he slammed the top of his head trying to scramble underneath. Vel grabbed his head and howled in pain and exasperation as the beast crashed into the wall. Grunting and cussing, Vel forced himself to his feet without checking his hands for blood, vaulting over the desk and making a break for it.

Shouldering the doors wide open, he ducked to the side and started to flee down the length of the building, down the line of plants that he had held conversation with moments earlier. The truck with finger prints on the hood was in the parking lot, but Vel didn't stop. Unless he had another plan up his sleeve, which he very much did not, the sands in his hourglass lasted for as long as he could outrun the beast.

The beast broke through the doors. He could not outrun it.

All he could do was flatten himself against the building when the beast lunged. Its shaggy fur, coarse with wire-like tendrils, flew past him so close it whipped his shirt. When he tried to double back he tripped and fell into the plants, splitting the skin of his jaw against the rocks at their roots. He yelped, scrambling to make himself small, thinking maybe he could scurry like a mouse underneath the plant cover but knowing he couldn't. The beast snarled over him, its image shrouded by the plants' branches.

The sound of a car pulled up and everything froze for a moment. The car door, someone getting out, slamming it shut.

Lieu's voice, from way over near the front of the clinic, called his name in cautious alarm.

Vel, staring at the beast and panting madly, made a snap decision.

"*Lieu!!*" he screamed, "*Lieu over here, help!!*"

The beast snarled and swiped down. Vel flinched, hearing wood and leaves snap and shear clean off. Then three, four, five punchy sounds cracking against the parking lot. Vel flinched again, his hands hovering over his ears. Another gunshot.

Then the beast hit the ground with one last thunderous tremor.

Lieu's footsteps ran up, stopping just short of the beast's body. Vel cautiously lifted his head, then crawled from between the plants and the building wall.

"Vel, what the hell are you doing here?" Lieu panted. All other questions she could ask were wrapped up within that one, but he could tell they were there just from the intensity of her glare. He grimaced getting up and almost lost his balance from the sudden sharp pains in his leg. His hand brushed along the wounded edges of the plants, and he kept it there in apology.

"Good question," he managed to reply, "Uh, I saw it through. Just like you expected."

Lieu straightened her stance when it was clear the immediate danger was gone. Rather, she straightened her stance now that she was able to focus all her ire on him. Now, she could say *this isn't what I meant* all she wanted, but what was she going to do? Tell Vel to stop being Vel? Much as it exasperated her she was one of the only people that never pushed that issue. For better or for worse. This, of course, was for the worse. Or better. He couldn't decide.

Always stuck in the middle.

"A panic call coming from the same address you text me moments later warrants explanation, *Velasquez*."

Vel let out a breath of pain as he leaned against the building. Lieu meant it as a threat but he could almost laugh at the use of his full name. Almost.

The corpse of the beast made him swallow all his laughter with a sobering sense of knowledge, both of what he had done and how he would not tell Lieu the whole truth.

16

The rest of the night was slow, sluggish enough to feel like a damnation. Vel sat on the edge of the curb while Lieu's backup arrived. He answered what he could about the discrepancy in the files left in Dr. Thompson's office and his suspicion that they were all linked. But despite Thompson's truck being there, the good doctor himself wasn't found. Vel confessed he didn't know why, but maybe it would have something to do with what a Luminol test would turn up on that thing.

As for the beast, he stared at its unmoving body. Lieu had commented that with research they might be able to link it to the death of Laura. Vel didn't respond. Whether that had pinged in Lieu's mind as strange regardless of the ways Laura's death had ruined him he didn't look to find out.

The pendant was forever lodged in the beast's belly, and with its death it would never revert to the human it once was. Vel would keep it that way. It felt like a dark and horrible decision, but he had already gambled everything expecting to die or worse. Reckless. Laura wouldn't approve. Not even a Laura from the grave.

Mice could only run so far as the time they bought allowed them.

As a medic dabbed at the spot on his head where a concussion was surely brewing, Vel lost himself to thought. Thompson was

155

a killer first and foremost, getting his kicks from slaughtering women that were his patients. Did he enjoy that they were white, or did he enjoy that the men they loved weren't? That the men, brown and darker, wouldn't be able to fight Thompson because if they stepped the least bit out of line Thompson's word would come out on top and none of their white partners would be alive to vouch for their anger? He thought of Jean, how he covered his accent to speak on the phone, how it seemed all so respectable, how his slip-ups ran so deep to the heart Vel almost felt like he shouldn't hear them. What had that done to Jean, he wondered—and what had it done to him with Chelsea's murder?

Or was it all just truly random? Because if it was, then Laura's pendant really did protect her and whatever other victims Thompson would've chosen down the line. Turning him into the monster he was on the inside. Turning his mind bestial to buy Vel time to escape not once but twice. Disrupting the pattern, making Vel notice out of the frustration of being dismissed. Making him obsess. As much as that obsession nearly killed him.

His faith in his power felt juvenile and untempered now, seeing the destruction it wrought upon someone he stupidly tried to protect without figuring out how. Or rather, someone he left magic to protect instead of himself.

No.

Thompson would've killed her anyway. He had to tell himself that otherwise madness would truly take him and he would never emerge from his sorrow.

The case of the axe-murdered women went cold with Thompson's disappearance. At the very least the families had some closure on who the killer was. The beast was determined to be a rabid escaped grizzly bear. That they gave no other details out made Vel think that he had spooked them good with it, notching the creature's existence into the hats of conspiracy enthusiasts.

When he told Jean that Chelsea's killer wouldn't be killing again, he refused to elaborate. Jean thought long and hard, processing the words. There was a grave, fearful respect that was both low and calculated in his voice when he thanked him. Vel's gut started to sink, and it occurred to him while he had introduced himself to Jean he had not exactly revealed all his credentials. Credentials that were easy enough to find through his advertisements in the yellow pages. *Private Investigator of the Strange and Unexplained.* Vel got the feeling that Jean had made the connection moreso than most, in particular with things he knew from Louisiana. Something akin to Hoodoo, something dangerous if prodded the wrong way.

Not that he had any ground to protest that now. Of course that meant it cut Vel off from asking for a good Creole recipe to cook, but he tried not to complain. His appetite was still fraught anyway.

A week after the beast's death and six days after the concussion cleared, Vel stopped by Shoua's. Her apartment was swathed over with construction and caution tape with reinforcing materials to the side. In the flurry of police reports her landlord was finally doing something to mitigate the flooding. It wouldn't help too much with the fact that she was on the edge of a flood plain, but it was better than nothing—and it kept her from him.

Vel did not cross the threshold of her apartment, sheepishly unsticking his knife from the door and setting the effigy wreath against his shins. Shoua watched from behind the couch. The same one he had fucked up on, the same one that irreparably damaged their friendship—as if there was anything to salvage without Laura, anyway.

Part of him *wanted* to salvage something. Laura had been one too many a loved one for Vel to lose, so even the barest of connections felt like a monumentally heart-wrenching loss. It was hard to tell if Shoua felt the same, but though her silence was as unbreakable as stone she didn't shoo him away.

His voice cracked, dry, and decided upon logistics for conversation, "When's the work gonna be done?"

"Door goes in tomorrow," she answered, "They're digging holes around the windows and caulking everything." Shoua paused as if to wait for him to make a horrible pun, but when he didn't she shifted her grip on herself. Vel guessed it was her version of relaxing.

"Your stuff is uh," he gestured at the empty areas in her apartment, struggling to find foundation, "Whenever you wanna pick it up."

Shoua nodded.

He reached down to touch the effigy, bracing himself to leave, "Shoua, um...," Vel looked away, biting the inside of his cheek, "I'm sorry. Thanks for putting up with me these past—god, two months."

Shoua then looked away, indicating the hint of emotion he had feared had been missing. But it was there, buried, yes, but there. Out of the corner of his eye he saw her swallow as if preparing to speak, maybe to say the same at him. It was a struggle. It always had been, and now it was worse.

"Let me know if...if you need anything, Boots," he said it gently, sincerely, past the pain in his throat, "I think I'm finally gonna lay low for a while."

"Finally?" she asked, meaning for it to be biting. Normalcy.

The corner of his lip curled up.

"On purpose this time."

Instead of sniffing dismissively she adjusted again and said, "Right."

Right.

"Take care," he bid, and then loud enough so she could not mistake to hear it, "Please."

"You too." It was quieter than he had said it, but he tilted his head in acknowledgment as he backed out of her apartment and closed the broken door.

17

The doorbell rang and Vel jogged over, his heart in his throat. It was a terrible mixture, wanting to put up a good face, knowing he couldn't, wanting honesty to win over. He took a deep breath, scrunched his eyes tight, then opened the door to Laura's parents.

Mr. Piper was tall—not to Vel, but to everyone else—with a head set back by his snow-white beard and glasses sitting far down his nose. He was bigger than Vel, though, with thick hands and short fingers. Laura had told him she loved watching her father's hands work on wood and carpentry. The skin on his palms was so thick that he could shave off splinters with them, smoothing edges so that it seemed he only ever used the finer grades of sandpaper. He was a quiet man described as stubborn by his wife, but amiably so. He hated driving unless the conditions were near perfect, and now as the monsoons were finally starting to dwindle he agreed to come down from Prescott to visit. (Of course, his wife reminded him, the haboobs were still being kicked up, but to a man that lived in sawdust that was home.)

Mrs. Piper looked closer to Laura, average height, same laugh, same inflections of the voice. She still had color to her hair, streaked with grays that fell in a comfortable mess from the bun set high on her head. Unlike Mr. Piper her complaints were out loud—until he interjected and she told him to *pipe down, Piper*, before continuing her personal Olympic sport. But she was a lovely woman that complained about the right sorts of things, petty or otherwise, and was never seen without a splash of color on her person. She had held many jobs over the years to her own delight, taking work home to marvel at the differences from one job to the next. It had helped Laura be comfortable with being a realtor now with the knowledge she could change later. That hurt to think about.

Both parents greeted him warmly, in a loud sort of way that was in reality masking with volume. Vel accepted their hug, trying to return the tone but already struggling with his mask. Still he invited them inside as his voice slipped into hushed anguish.

They had come to see the house their daughter had bought now that she was dead. Though he was grateful to see them again and not in funerary attire, he was wracked with anxious nerves. Yes his name was on the mortgage, but ultimately the decision laid with the folks who helped Laura buy the property in the first place. On top of that there was the topic of her life insurance—it had seemed so premature at the time, but then so many other things seemed premature now after the fact. He should be grateful her father was as stubborn as he was.

But he wasn't family, not officially, not on the books. The insurance went to them, as it should, and the idea of discussing the money when so egregiously bereaved—Vel could barely stomach it. He'd make it no matter what, he had made it without Laura before and with a much worse sense of the world. And Lieu hadn't completely cut him off either. He'd make it.

Still, Vel was not prepared for that conversation, even though he knew they'd be coming down eventually.

After formalities that Vel barely made it through, they started to leisurely wander the house. With luck he had most of the mess from the beast cleaned up, though the window stuck if he tried to open it now and he had yet to actually replace the door to the spare bedroom—there were only the hinges on the frame to suggest what had been in place.

But *his* mess, there were plenty of vestiges of that. Vel awkwardly snatched a food bag from the coffee table and crunched it in his hands, feeling ashamed.

"Sorry I—cleaned up a little but I...," he packed the garbage tighter in his hand, "I didn't want to uh, lie. About how it's been."

Laura's parents stood quietly in the living room, the only real sound coming from the crumbling paper bag and the rattling beak-clacking of a roadrunner that was making its way through the backyard. Mrs. Piper stepped forward.

"We figured as much...," it was said gently, without assumption and trying not to step on his feet. Vel stared glumly at the table, squeezing the bag once more before ducking away to toss it. Upon returning he saw he backs of Laura's parents looking elsewhere, surveying the space where he lived. Where she used to live. Against his will he knew that it was an image that would sear in his mind for the rest of his life. He snuck back in front of them, standing at the edge of the hallway to the bedrooms. Her parents remained quiet.

"It's a good house," her carpenter father commented after a while of touring the rest. Vel nodded dumbly. After a beat he added, "We can tell Laura was very serious about you."

Vel nodded harder and struggled to speak past the choking pit in his throat, "Yeah I, I was serious about her too." It was then that he noticed that tears were leaking out, and he brushed a thumb in the corners of his eyes. Unfortunately for him, each attempt to dam his tears made more appear. Frustration and anxiety didn't help, and inside he was yelling at himself to get his composure together. He had to. It was serious, he *had* to.

Something moved in his vision and he stiffened, even when he realized it was Mrs. Piper. Her eyes, thankfully hazel and unlike Laura's, were sympathetic, "We talked to Shoua briefly. She...warned isn't quite the right word. Told us how hard it's been for you."

"It's...gotten a little bit better," he weakly lied.

"So it goes," Mrs. Piper nodded as she assessed him head to toe. At the very least he wasn't wearing dirty clothes.

"Vel," Mr. Piper cut in, folding his broad hands in front of him, "To be blunt, it won't get better." Vel looked at him, realizing that he was avoiding eye contact and adjusting his glasses. His voice was not cruel nor accusatory despite its leveled delivery. He sighed, heavy from the belly, and said, "Not all the way."

Vel nodded. Laura's mother frowned.

"Uh," Vel ripped the bandage off, "About the mortgage,"

Mrs. Piper gave a disgusted scoff, "Honey, you're on the paperwork!"

"Aren't you too, now? As inheritors."

"And?" she challenged, hands on her hips just like Laura used to do, "And what?"

Mr. Piper's hand set calmly on his wife's shoulder, tagging in, "The insurance is more important to discuss."

Vel bobbed his head again, wincing that it was how he was getting through this, "Shouldn't there be an, uh, lawyer present?"

"Eventually," Mr. Piper agreed, "But let's get it all straight before that. How much of it do you need?"

Vel short-circuited. Furrowing his brow, he stared in blank confusion before stuttering, "I...don't know what you mean."

"Vel, for chrissakes, we *have* everything already," Mrs. Piper's complaining voice was out, once again about the right thing with funny fervor, "Laura found this house. Laura loved this house, and she loved you. We can agree on that, right?"

"Right, but,"

"*No*," Mrs. Piper interjected, firm but gentle, "No, no, no, no. We have no need of the house. If you want to move that's alright, we understand. But we'd like for you to keep living here, with any help that you need. Right, Piper?"

Laura's father nodded.

Overwhelmed, Vel thought he was swimming as he struggled to process what was being said. Once, twice he stuttered then choked on his own words. The Pipers politely waited for him to regain himself, watching as tears rolled down his cheeks. When he gave up trying to respond, Mrs. Piper filled in again.

"And...about Thanksgiving. If you've nowhere to go, give us a call, won't you?"

Vel nodded, tried to maintain eye contact, squeezed his eyes shut.

"In the meantime, we'll figure out what you need and take us all to get it settled then. Yes?" Mr. Piper peered over his glasses, a move that he was used to doing with people shorter than him but looked cartoonish when he was looking up at Vel.

"Yes," he managed to whisper, "Thank you."

Mrs. Piper finally closed the distance she had been itching to close and wrapped him in a hug, "She wouldn't want a beautiful home to sit empty, you know."

"I know," Vel replied.

"Thank you for being good to her."

It pierced, pierced deep in a way he hoped wasn't obvious. Or that his wincing could be taken as crying. If only he had been better to her, more of something, less of other things, something complete instead of trite.

But her parents didn't seem to look at him as so many halves, and Laura didn't either. Occasionally they *had* gotten into fights about that, mostly because Laura could not see one as a shortcoming of the other. If he was so mixed, Witch and Catholic, Mexican and mystery Indigenous, surely it meant something beautiful instead of something tormented. That's how she saw it, unwillingly steamrolling Vel's insecurities by doing so.

Though there was a blunt sort of love in her assumptions of his beauty as he was, and there were times he deeply appreciated her for it. And here, from her parents, after fuck-up after fuck-up after fuck-up, he needed it. Mrs. Piper hugged him like one whole person.

He hugged her back, "Thank you for Laura."

About the Author

Bre lives with her cat in an apartment very far away from the state of Arizona and deserts; although it's true that the desert runs deep in half of her heritage. Certainly this isn't a metaphorical leap in discussing identity or anything. Approach Bre in the wild with boisterous joy and be met with in kind, but be wary that she's almost always watching a gross horror film.